Stardust,
7-Eleven,
Route 57,
A&W,
and *So Forth*

Stardust,
7-Eleven,
Route 57,
A&W,
and *So Forth*

STORIES BY

Patricia Lear

ALFRED A. KNOPF   NEW YORK   1992

THIS IS A BORZOI BOOK
PUBLISHED BY ALFRED A. KNOPF, INC.

"Ironman," "Hot," "Graceland," "Solace," "Licensed for Private Exhibition Only," and "Powwow" were first published in *The Quarterly*. "After Memphis" was first published in *The Antioch Review*. "Powwow" was reprinted in *Prize Stories 1991: The O. Henry Awards*.

Library of Congress Cataloging-in-Publication Data
Lear, Patricia [date]
Stardust, 7-Eleven, Route 57, A & W, and So Forth : Stories / Patricia Lear.
—1st ed.
p. cm.
Contents: Ironman—Solace—Hot—Graceland—After Memphis— Angels—Licensed for privated exhibition only— Powwow.
ISBN 0-394-57998-4
I. Title.
PS3562.E237R68 1992
813'.54—dc20   91-18972
                                                      CIP

Manufactured in the United States of America

Published April 4, 1992
Second Printing, April 1992

FOR BILL AND PETER AND MERRITT

I am deeply grateful to United Airlines Frequent Flyer Program, the man who kept upgrading me at the Hotel Wales, dear Gordon Lish, the Corporation of Yaddo, the O. Henry Awards, that angel Betsy Rachal. Also, I wish to thank Jimmy Rogers, Dorothy and Bob Lear, Suzanne McNear, Janie MacLean, Jim Cavanaugh, The Performance Group, Stephani Cook, Alan Wolf, Connie, Barbara, Margie, Mark, and Mrs. John Pumphrey, who lived in Memphis and sent me money.

—P.L.

Contents

IRONMAN   3

AFTER MEMPHIS   15

HOT   49

GRACELAND   55

SOLACE   67

ANGELS   119

LICENSED FOR PRIVATE
    EXHIBITION ONLY   137

POWWOW   147

Stardust,
7-Eleven,
Route 57,
A&W,
and *So Forth*

Ironman

I am recently living at Lloyd's with Lloyd and his dog Blackie. Lloyd is my young lover of an Asian background, and Blackie is a decent dog somebody else probably used to own. With the windows thrown wide and the desert stars outside showing through punch holes in the night sky, Blackie sleeps curled around on herself with Lloyd and me in the king-sized water bed, and she bobs there down at the foot of the bed on a collection of Indian blankets we keep ready in case of cold.

How it usually goes in the early mornings is Lloyd kicking the old comforter off the bed where it clumps up down on the floor with the goose down squashed flat, and then us getting our running clothes on and lacing up our high-tech, state-of-the-art, gel-cushioned training shoes and slapping out the side screen porch door with Blackie snaking out through the first crack of unfettered sunlight either of us makes in the door and her firing off like a rifle shot chasing through the weeds.

Lloyd and I follow. We trot gently up to the path high in the hills to warm up, shaking out our arms and legs as we go along, winding and doing hairpin crookbacks and nice banked turns up close by on hard-packed clay. When the path straightens out and we get going and ease into our real run, one and then the other one of us has to fight off Blackie for the lead, which has some danger in it because Blackie has a problem with jumping and nipping with her tiny front teeth.

Talk about horizons. At the break of dawn when the sun rollers color up over the running hills in clear soft shapes, we are looking at the whole world from up there on our early-morning runs, running with our feet low, kicking along the ground, and thinking only about our breathing, or which way we might want to go to next. In this way, we pack in anywhere from a twelve- to twenty-miler, six solid days a week.

Okay, I got to say it now, something you don't need to know if you are a woman like me or will want to hear about if you are a man like my husband Moss is, but young guys are nice, and to me a better thing than living with an old man your own age. Things crash around and there are wild tricks. There is an off-balance quality to our life—Lloyd's and Blackie's and mine. None of us matches. In other ways, of course, we do, we do, we really do.

Okay. We listen to a rock station on the radio in Lloyd's old piece of shit of a car, and I believe in and like most of the songs. When we make love, Lloyd and I, we use our whole flat open hands over our whole flat open bodies. We use our mouths. We even roll Blackie, old weird Blackie, over on her back and kiss her stomach and take deep sniffs of her neck fur. We scoot Blackie over to give us some room and I do things like crawl between Lloyd's legs and hang tail-to-the-wind off his side. We aren't afraid to try things is what I mean. Then we sleep, then we run, then we eat, and that's about it; that's our little life.

Well, I say our life makes easily as much sense as mine and my husband Moss's ever did or even what I can figure out from watching other people in their lives.

Moss would stuff his fingers in his ears if he heard me talking about my life now, that it could be any better than being with him plus my little piddling jaunts to the Workout World.

I am now a triathlete, among about one other thing, and when my mom sees the senior female bodybuilders on week-end TV (they are everywhere now), she calls me up and she says, "What in the world, Crystal, just what in the world? Those silly women, you don't want to look like those women, do you, Crystal?"

Well, yes, surprise! surprise! I think I do. I am beginning to like more and more what I see when I see those women, and when I tell my mom this, she has been known to hang up on me. What she needs to understand is that her daughter's eye for beauty is undergoing a transformation.

What I have been working on these past couple of years is really getting a grip on things. It has been important to be pushing to the edge of things. There was a point at the tail end of the being-together part of our marriage, Moss's and mine, where my life measured about an inch, registered a zero on the Richter scale. It was all I could do just to get out of bed in the mornings, sometimes just so I could get back in it for the rest of the day until it was time to get back out again. I would smoke cigarettes and drink grapefruit juice and try to sleep dressed in the spandex and leggings from the one thing I did. Moss would be saying, his wife pinioned to the bed with an ache in her soul, he would say, "Well, that's tough, babe." Then Moss would have to go on out to earn us a living, smelling of his Christmas-present aftershave. He would go out into the world and drive to his office or drive to a meeting, or he would pull on some pineapple-patterned golf pants and throw his clubs in the back of the car to earn us a living doing business with customers on the golf course. So here's what I did.

Baby-cakes, what I did was I did the Ironman. Me. I did that.

Life has ways of being hard for all of us. It has been hard on Lloyd, with his pearly skin and funny English, and even on Blackie, who has tar-colored bare skin patches on her where her fur will no longer grow anymore. She is probably an older dog—I don't know how many years exactly—but even if she is a young dog, she clearly has had a hard life. More than anything, I would kind of like to know exactly what happened to Blackie so I could quit thinking of things, envisioning things—sadistic tortures, cruel abandonments, hit-and-run car accidents—and so I could make all the needed exceptions for her bad habits, such as her endless barking, and give her all the necessary time to come around to a deeper trust. What I do for Blackie is I let her, as I said, sleep with Lloyd and me, and I give her long runs over the mountains and spend extra money on some scientific dog food the vet says is the best.

But, as you know, there is always going to be something. This is real life, not heaven. You don't really just do the Iron-man and find yourself a young boyfriend and have that be it, have it be the last thing, have the hard times be all nice and neat and behind you. With life, like ocean swimming, there's waves and undercurrents and good days and bad days and . . . you never know.

The facts are that for a while now, I won't be going out in the mornings with Lloyd and Blackie on our early-morning runs. The facts are that for a while now there won't be any strapping on the little ankle weights and doing distance, any intervals or any fartlek, no down on the beach running back-wards and running forwards, no visits with the foot doctor, no signing up for races, no scrambling up the hills and scrambling back down the hills, kicking up storms of dust with rocks and cinders mixed in. The facts are that Lloyd'll be leaving me back in the bed while he and Blackie slap out the screen door, just the two of them, sort of like fuckhead Moss used to do when Moss would be going off someplace or throwing his golf clubs into the back of the car. You see, what happened was that eight days, seven hours, and twenty-four minutes ago, while doing my hill work, I slid off a hill. Lloyd was with me. Blackie had chased off barking like the stupid-dog dumb-shit she can at times be. The rest, however you imagine the rest, is the way it was.

Eileen is the woman I found in the Yellow Pages after I saw what I was going to be doing was just lying out here on my back in the chaise longue or curved into the canvas butterfly chair under the firecracker tree getting out of the way of myself. I mean, she is the one I have my phone consultations with, or sessions with, or whatever you want to call them. She was the one on the other end of the Help Hotline the first time I called. Her full name is Eileen-something-something-Jewish, plus some degree, and one of the things I've been discussing with Eileen is how I think I don't do at all well anymore just lying places.

To which Eileen says, "Crystal, you healed your life once. You can do it again."

To which I say to Eileen, "Eileen, it's too hard. I can't go through all that saving of myself again."

Back with Moss, it was in a movie theater with my leg pulled over Moss's leg, never touching the popcorn once, not one single kernel, never seeing the movie either, that I started thinking. The lights went down, and by the time the previews were over, I was loose from the world and off in my head picking at my life's scabs, just fingernailing them up and getting the blood to flow and looking at what it was that was driving me so crazy. The things I found would just make me think love more, think life more, while Moss was sitting there watching the movie and reaching his hand into my jeans to walk his fingers around in there. And his hand was not romance, either. I do not know what it was, but it was not romance or love, either. And you know what? I still cannot figure out what to do about that, either—you know, that it wasn't.

We make plans in the mornings. Being newly confined as I am, I have come to notice what I never really looked at and noticed before. Such as Lloyd himself.

Eileen says about him, when I bring it up with her in our phone sessions with what she calls sheer wonderment in my voice, Eileen says, "Well, Crystal, look who's there with him. Think about that and we will talk some more tomorrow."

Mornings go like this now. Us all awake. Blackie zinging through all the rooms of the house. Lloyd lacing up his running shoes, keeping Blackie at bay with an elbow, Lloyd's ears girlish, showing through splits in his hair. Together, dog and man trot out to the path, and I watch them as far as I can see them go, me wrapped in an Indian blanket from my place in the upstairs bed.

I get in the tub pretty much on schedule—just like I had a schedule. Then Blackie shows up first to lap water out of the toilet. Lloyd comes in next, glistening and slick and wiping his brow off with his wadded shirt, then dropping his clothes to pool on the floor, kicking the pile over to soak up where I have sloshed water over the sides of the tub. I look at his ankles, how hard things inside his ankles move as Lloyd shifts his weight, barefooted and hunched over while brushing his teeth or even while taking long foot-long pulls back through his hair with my wide-tooth wooden comb before he disappears down the hall to the shower.

Since it has quit raining, in the mottled shade of the firecracker tree I sit grasshopper-positioned in the canvas butterfly chair doing what they tell me to do. I am fighting sliding into that crevice between how things are and how I want them to be and mentally am trying to make up a list of things to discuss with Eileen when it is our scheduled time to talk. I keep the cordless lying out here next to me on the bricks, and after a while I kind of, how you do, sit blurred and unfocused . . . I bog down.

Maybe this is what depression is.

Blackie goes nuts with barking, which means nothing to me, means squirrel or garbage man or leaf—such is Blackie—but I do feel the tickling of something brushing my forehead. Could be anything, but there is also breathing as well, so I focus my eyes and see my husband Moss's face above me.

"Thought I'd make a courtesy call in person on the shut-in," Moss says (over Blackie's barking like a maniac), while pulling himself up straight and holding up like two bowling pins two glass bottles of Coke swinging loose in his free hand, his fingers just lightly pinching their frosty necks.

Moss drops down on the redwood bench next to my butterfly chair and shoves all my magazines off onto the bricks of the patio. "Business trip," he says as he puts one hand under his chin and unbunches the fingers to tap on his cheekbone. "Ramada Inn," he says.

On my blaster is playing one of those teenage songs about smoking joints and rolling around on top of women, and Blackie is still up on her feet, still suspicious and giving out little half barks through her rubbery lips.

"What did I ever do to you, Crystal?" Moss says, looking to me like he just got out of the barber shop, with his hair clipped short and spiky with something wet. Then he stands up, setting the takeout bag on the end of the bench, and turns and goes up the stairs to the kitchen.

I yell after him, "Hey! I don't eat this stuff. Leave anything you brought for me right in the bag, Moss."

Moss waves me off, kind of fluttering a hand behind him as he peels off his suit jacket and twirls it around his shoulders in a way I never saw him do before. His white shirt sticks to a spot in the middle of his back.

Next I see Moss up there violating the serenity of Lloyd's hand-rubbed-by-my-hands white-pine kitchen, slamming drawers and getting glasses and cracking ice-cube trays and pulling sheets of paper towel off a roll next to the sink. "We got to talk, babe," Moss says, a paper towel easing through the air to settle itself undersea-like on the floor, Moss leaning into the doorjamb with just his upper body, still busy messing with something in front of him on the counter. I am getting my arms and legs arranged and mentally negotiating my mind around my amazing pain and then standing myself up smack into the center of the pain so I can hobble up the stairs and wedge past Moss, saying, "Bathroom," to him, and then I go on upstairs to put in a call to Eileen on the cordless I carry up there with me. I say, "Get Eileen," to whoever's taking calls on the Hotline, all the time trying to occupy myself with envisioning Eileen's face.

I envision Eileen completely different every time.

I lie down on the water bed to wait for her return call; sometimes it takes a couple of minutes and sometimes if she is away, sometimes it takes a very long time. I do a few of my leg raises and pelvic tilts for my back, scared to tie up the line with calling Lloyd where he works selling sleeping bags and mountain-trek-adventure supplies, though I would like to do just that, call Lloyd and call Eileen both. Blackie is on me like a flash, tussling around and tidal-waving the bed. I fend her off with my foot.

Eileen says, when she calls back, "Oh, that's wonderful, Crystal. It's a circus, it's a circus! What an opportunity!" Then Blackie jumps on me again and Moss comes to the bottom of the stairs and says my name. I take two sticks of gum from the bedside table and carefully unwrap them and accordion them up neatly before I put them in my mouth. I hobble back down the stairs and back past Moss and go outside, where I lower myself into the chaise, keeping my arms elbow-locked as long as I can and lowering myself by taking the weight as much as possible with my shoulders.

I see Moss is walking back down the steps carrying a tray, and his big white shirt is inflating out from his suit pants in places where the wind gets in.

"You've done it now, Crystal," he says. "Tell me. What all *have* you done to yourself, Crystal?"

He wolfs his piled-up hot dog, tearing off small pieces for Blackie and throwing them overhanded to the farthest corner of the patio, and then he eats the hot dog he expected I would eat, plus all of the French fries too.

The sun in the sky begins to fade as it does at that time of day, and Moss says to me, "I think it's kind of funny. I'm kind of impressed with you actually, Crystal," he says.

Then he says to me, as I watch him stand up and do a final little practice swing like he had a golf club in his hand, "You know, Crystal, this whole thing should bother me. I don't know why it doesn't bother me—because it should. But it doesn't."

We can almost see the roof of the Ramada from here, from where Lloyd and Blackie and I have got ourselves in our water bed at all of ten o'clock of a night. We are sitting in the dark without the TV on or even our eerie lava light, just a little desert moon to flesh out our outlines.

Lloyd is buck naked and yellowish, leaning up against some feather pillows he has jammed up hard against the head-board, and there are two hanks of his hair sliding down over his shoulders and glowing softly just like I want them to be. He's out of a fantasy, man, like satin sheets look spilling off beds in Moss's *Penthouse* magazines; none of us ever actually has had satin sheets to spill but I've had Lloyd. I am in my underpants, and Lloyd has pulled me up against him by wrapping one arm around my rib cage and heaving me up so I am laid against him on a slant, like I was laid out in the chaise longue all day long out back of the house, healing. Lloyd sticks one hand between my legs and looks out at the moon.

Blackie is standing up on all fours walking around the bed and stopping to bark in obnoxious little rapid-fire bursts of dog-bark out through the window—I guess at the lights of the Ramada, where Moss is probably in the lounge by now seated at a little square table with a Rob Roy watching the show they put on there on Thursday nights. There is a girl singer.

Just knowing Moss is down there makes me uneasy. I imagine Moss floating up here and wreathing around us, like the smoky incense in the clay holder shaped like a tepee we picked up down in Santa Fe I got going across the room burning on Lloyd's old scratched-up bureau.

I tell Lloyd what's on my mind and he says . . . oh, hell, he doesn't care about Moss. Moss doesn't care about us. Moss isn't any big thing.

Next Moss has taken to, on a regular basis, crunching up our road with rolls and coffee in his business attire after Lloyd is off to the mountain store, or Moss will come after a breakfast meeting at the Ramada or after a lunch function or in the late afternoons with some champagne or some kind of wine and plastic cups. He brought a medium-sized ice sculpture day before yesterday. Also some little salmon-mousse canapés with capers on top from the same cocktail reception as the ice sculpture. Also there have been hard little sweet rolls with icing that Lloyd and I have been eating at night in bed, which came from a breakfast buffet.

Eileen said many things during our last phone consultation, while all this going back and forth was winding up and with me lying out back of Lloyd's in the firecracker shade with the cordless and huddled with a towel over my head, trying to find a comfortable position—and Moss upstairs packing up my things. I had said to Eileen, "What about the human dignity of love, Eileen?" but this one thing she never exactly answered, meaning—what about it, for me to figure it out. Or maybe I'd stumped her.

Back home with Moss, and while resting in the upstairs bed, when my mom called up I put it to her, you know, the same old thing—after we had worked through all the local-newsy news. I said to her, "What about the human dignity of love? What about love?" and my mom said, "What in the world, Crystal? Just what in the world? What is this thing you are trying to say?"

After Memphis

My big brother was the one who had lashed the Confederate flag to the antenna, and so there we were, the four of us, under the blaze of our banner, my brother and I two small heads sticking up proud in the back seat sucking on Popsicles—assuming we were ever noticed at all, which probably we weren't but maybe we were, by a gas station attendant or something—and with our dad's big company-president Cadillac tires rubbering us relentlessly North and with us inside with the car windows up and with the car doors locked so that when we fought and roughhoused we would not accidentally hit the door handle and fling outselves out. There was always around us a protective haze from our parents' cigarette smoke Spanish-mossing into drapey shapes in the corners.

In the night, after night fell, our parents were mostly just little red dots darting through the stillness of that hurtling tunnel of time that was all of us grinding on along on the old highways, our parents writing circles and S's and slashes with their cigarette ends that my brother and I could, you know, eye-blinkingly see from the back in the dark when we opened our eyes—but also, and mostly in their murmurings to each other, our parents were the only things standing between us and the stories they told each other about, us saying, "What, what, what?" when we couldn't hear a part or catch a name, and which stories were to us, of course, what life was about back then with a capital L.

Our mom had stayed on with us to finish the school year, like is often done, and she did the usual things that go with the waiting for the school year to be out—she took us to the pediatrician for our shots and kept being assistant leader for my Camp Fire Girls and took us to the swimming pool and put the house up for sale and went to exciting places like to the beauty parlor while we were in school, our daddy already having gone on ahead of us across the Mason-Dixon line and taken out bank loans and all, spending a year getting things going such as starting his company and finding us a house and then coming back to chip us with a chisel out of the South, haul us with a crane out of the country-club swimming pool— which is how he said it was for him from the way we were acting.

And with us packed by his own hands into the back seat with the line taped down the middle in red tape, also by him, so that we would not fight or start the next Civil War by touching each other, our dad made a beeline straight through downtown Memphis to get it over with, to speed us as fast as possible across that bridge over the Mississippi River, since my brother and I were suddenly swamped emotionally with a great South-ern pride-flowering that had started us singing and yelling "Dixie" and soon me hanging out the windows, screaming, just nothing but pure screaming.

I had just gotten old enough to care about the South, which was really just as everybody was packing up around me for the move. My brother cared first, of course, and then me. In the car my brother was occasionally shrieking out, "Why, why, why?" between "Dixie" verses, so our mom had to say to us that if we were happy people, we could be happy people anywhere, and our dad, who was landing us in West Memphis, Arkansas, down in the industrial section of town (after lots of stoplight and direction readings from our mom and after the usual gas station phone calls to the place we were trying to get to), down at the visitor parking lot of the Razorback Ice Cream Company, our dad said it was up to us in this life as far as he knew and not the other way around.

And this was the exact day in West Memphis, Arkansas, right after we left the Razorback Ice Cream Company, that was the last time we ever were as kids to have our birthright Memphian accents, and it was the first time we ever knew we even had Memphian accents in the first place. It was from that day on in West Memphis, Arkansas, from where our dad had threaded our way out of the industrial section of town, it was from lunch of that exact first day in West Memphis, Arkansas, that I think our accents started eroding. I believe it began while we were ordering our Rebel Dogs from the Yankee-looking waitress and while, waiting to eat and unawares, we started absorbing the intonations of the speech of everybody sitting around us.

It was just business that we all ate ice cream—Peanut Buster Parfaits, little Dixie cups, regular ice-cream sandwiches, Cremesicles, Bomb Pops, Drumsticks. You name it, we probably sampled some of it, as our father went zigzagging us from ice-cream store to ice-cream factory (the Razorback only the first) through Tennessee, Arkansas, and Missouri to teach himself everything he could about the processing and the business end of the ice-cream business and to sit around swapping ideas with the other novelty ice-cream company presidents and take us all on long, lengthy tours of manufacturing and production areas, storage and freezer space, shipping dock and on-site lunchroom and convenience vending machines, even snaking us single file through the front office to meet management and to chat with the secretarial and clerk-typist pool. We would drink bottles of pop and listen to the men talking about sugar prices and overruns, milk solids and packaging, as our mom chatted with one of the employee ladies and drank from a paper cone of coffee that was fitted into a little plastic-handled holder.

At night, though, we mixed business with pleasure by staying only in motels with swimming pools, where water bugs frog-legged around in the water with us. Back on the road, we discussed the Civil War and how they had it all wrong in the history books, especially with regards to what we were up to and what they *really* were up to. They did not care about our slaves and our slaves' freedom and their welfare at all. They were just jealous of how good we were doing. They just wanted our raw materials, is what it was. Us plantation owners were left with nothing, no help to keep our crops and cotton going without our slaves, which we loved and cared for.

And the slaves, hell, they even had it worse free than with us!

I was feeling a deep personal unfairness done to me and was getting madder and madder about wanting our slaves back, as well as the life that went along with us having them, and it was then that my brother brought up with great suspicion, "Hey, how soon is it anyway, or how late is it exactly, that the state of Missouri, where we are moving to, joined in with the Confederacy, and how is it that Kansas never joined in, though it wavered for about a minute, but in the end, what's the deal with Kansas going blue, not gray?"

"Don't know, don't care," our father said, driving us up

through the Ozark Mountains at this point and impressing the hillbillies with our company-president Cadillac flying the Confederate flag. "Anyway, all that is over," he said, pointing out a big truck passing us going the opposite way on the highway with his own name emblazoned across its big side. "Anyway, all that is over," our dad said once again. "Especially the old moldy old Civil War." Then he asked our mom to hand us over into the back seat some rolled-up floor plans and a sketch of what our new house could look like once it was finished—although they had yet to decide exactly on which front to put on it from the choices available: Ranch, French Provincial, or Antebellum.

It was the floor plans and housefront choices my brother and I spread out across us in the back seat that got me to remembering my giant drawing book I carried with me everywhere to draw in, and after fixing the elasticized shoulders on my peasant blouse that had snapped up, I was soon busying myself with my artwork—I was drawing plantation houses with pillars standing across the front and drawing also cotton fields with slaves. On other pages tucked away, I have to admit, there were pages and pages of penises, like on my brother and on our dog we used to have, and then on other pages there were also a few very, very stylized vaginas as seen from the front—as in the mirror—and though I did these items in a very, very stylized way, that is what they *were*. So I was humming "Dixie" and drawing and was thinking about all the old times that I would not forget that we were leaving back in Tennessee—such as the lap, lap, lap of the country-club swimming pool electrically underlit after dark by a splintery light and top-lit by that magical Memphis moon and floated with a drizzle of fallen cottonwood blossoms (not ten thousand water bugs). Such as Elvis, barbecue pork sandwiches from the Pig 'N Whistle, polo ponies we could ride out in Germantown, the

Christmas Cotillion where someday I would be a debutante and look like Scarlett O'Hara because of not one thing I myself would ever have to have done.

But it was on the road that wends through Springfield, Missouri—the home of the Ozark Big Wheel Ice Cream Delight Sandwich—and on up through the Ozark Mountains and around the many finger lakes of the Lake of the Ozarks, which I remember clearly because it was about there, as we were suddenly coming up over a big surprise hill in the road that lifted us up into the air—my brother even said, "Is this us? The South rising again?"—that the truth of this move-we-did-not-want-to-make began seeping out sideways. I was sitting next to my brother, at first peacefully drawing more of what I said I was drawing in the back seat as the family talked on without me, more about the Civil War that I did not understand or care to learn about just then since unlike my brother I did have a limit to my caring about the teensiest details, and my brother was droning away with his head stuck up between our parents in the front seat, droning names and battles and summits and dates—my brother knew everything, every little detail, his caring knew no limits—so it was about then our dad cut it short finally and began telling us the usual stories about his Uncle Winn (so what) we had heard all our lives anyway and about "the farm" (so what) where this Uncle Winn lived. Our mom said, "Oh, Winn . . ." trailing off, but our dad talked on about this Uncle Winn and this farm where we were in fact going to be living until our house was finished being built, our dad telling us story after story as he hurtled us evermore deeper and farther into the North, the upchuck of all which was that it was because of this Uncle Winn was the reason we were all riding along so comfy in this Cadillac in the first place (so what) because it was from this Uncle Winn that our dad had learned the meaning of the word "work."

Our dad spoke about Uncle Winn in the same tones, I noticed, as my brother did when he was talking about Robert E. Lee or Jefferson Davis. He spoke about how Uncle Winn was the only one of anyone in our whole family to last through the Depression—no one else did, that is for sure, no one else did. "But how he had a temper," our dad said, "and when he lost it, watch out! You all remember I told you about the time when the stubborn mule refused to plow and Winn did the darnedest thing."

"Mule rocked the wrong boat there," our mom said, smiling back at me.

"It was the darnedest thing," our dad said.

Oh hell and so what. We had heard that mule story a million times, and I still never liked it. I was the kind of kid that could be made hysterical by such a story. I thought it was mean to the mule.

But just awestruck was our dad in the presence of this story, I could tell from his eyes glittering up in some approaching headlights, intent as he was with keeping that Cadillac hood ornament plowing a straight furrow North, back to where he was going to dip back into the same "good character" pond for some more of whatever it was that he had gotten back then for us all. And there was to be no way out, what with our mom, who I could see in plane-lit profile, nodding along with him, her eyes turning velvety and soft, her fingers working up his shoulder to his neck. Her stories were mostly aimed at me and were mostly about how not wanting anything was the only way to get anything, while our dad's were mostly aimed at my brother and were about how you just had to go out there and *get* anything if you were ever going to *have* anything.

Our dad said, "It was the darnedest thing."

Our mom said, "I'll swan."

I was sad all over again about the mule because I very much wanted a horse, and a mule was closer to being a horse than what I then had. I would have wanted to ride that mule. I would have taken good care of that mule, and he would have been pretty decrepit by now and old.

The first thing I remember from when we turned into the driveway of the farm and parked ourselves over by the barn was the rising of the sausage-commercial sun to the crowing of the sausage-commercial cocks, our dad having decided to push on and just get there, even though our mom said she could not sit anymore and had to go to the bathroom so bad she could "pop."

The second thing I remember is my brother in front of the barn, looming through the dawn from a place high up on a ladder, nails bristling from his teeth. I could see a big Confederate flag caped up over his shoulders and his hair ruffling along with the wheat crop in an early-morning breeze.

The third thing I remember is that there was an old barn turned dance studio right across the highway from the farm that had a spotlight dancer in a top hat and cane stuck up on the roof.

Uncle Winn was watching us all swarming in on him, watching us advancing up the yard from his rented hospital bed set up in the front parlor, us to him probably like *Night of the Living Dead* with our suitcases and left-over Popsicle wrappers and comic books and fistfuls of trip garbage we were made to clean out from the floor of the car, and me also with my blanket and pillow from the back seat.

Our dad was soon sitting in the pulled-up BarcaLounger, and those two!—our dad telling Winn—what was it?—something—it was something about butter-brickle ice cream back then our dad was all fired up about, just having cut a deal with Heath Bar to supply the butter-brickle part.

"Wait until you try it," our dad was saying to Winn. "It is the best thing you will ever eat," as Winn was saying, "What in the Sam Hill is that?" since he was staring out the picture window at my brother up on the ladder above the hayloft nailing in the last nail of our Confederate flag.

Winn sure would not be doing to any more mules what he had done to his own mule, I could see that from when I was made to go over and give him a kiss. The local Missouri mule population was safe from our dad's Uncle Winn at least.

Next morning it was "Up and at 'em, you all!" from our dad, who was dressed in his flight suit from the war when he bombed all the Germans, our dad who sang "Off we go into the wild blue yonder" like my brother and I sang "Dixie," who never slept much, though he would of if he could of, and who never found it in himself to do the thing, to do the sleep method that our mom always said worked for her, where you bore yourself to sleep is basically what you do. You lie in bed, and you get yourself and your arms and legs all settled how they feel best—you might want to try out a couple of positions first before choosing because here is the hard part—you *stay* in that same position. *No matter what.* Especially when the urge comes, *and it will,* to move or roll over, you by force of WILL *stay* in that same position. If you do this long enough, you are guaranteed by our mom of going to sleep. Our mom does this sleep method and says it works for her even on the night before Christmas. And the proof is in the pudding be-cause whenever I would go in to check on our mom in bed, such as if I was up going to the bathroom, there she would be, so calm and so asleep. Barely breathing.

Saying "Work time!" our dad was coming up the stairs to

our room and then kicking my brother's bed up on its right-side legs so it crashed down on the wood floor with my brother trying to stay asleep no matter what. My brother was going to cling to sleep next to me no matter what was done to him, me of course watching all this through flittery eyelashes and listening to my brother's breath breathing out Why's and I don't believe this's. Our dad was by this time finished with this part of his morning and was tromping on back downstairs to help Winn get going for the day, our dad doing what I know he did all that summer—lifting Winn gently up in his hospital bed, then leading Winn by the elbow over to the portapotty he had rolled in from the dining room, and then waiting in the kitchen for him, maybe making toast or reading some of the newspaper business section while he was waiting or maybe staying in the parlor with Winn but politely messing around with his back turned, spreading the covers over Winn's bed for him. All this while he was waiting, all while my brother would be stomping around my bed pulling all the chains on the antiquey lamps that we had in there and then going into the bathroom, door left wide open, never flushing, where he would sound like the mule must have sounded to Winn when the mule was going on some solid ground and Winn was stuck behind him waiting, hanging on to the plow.

My brother would suit up in his work coveralls—his T-shirt underneath peeping the Confederate flag through some unsnapped snaps—and he would sing "Dixie" like he thought if he could wake me up that would mean something, which it in no way meant anything as our mom was in charge of me, so him flinging his arms around and throwing his Eagle Scout slingshot to an end-on-end clatter across the wood floor before slamming out the door was just what I had to live with to get him the hell out of there in those summer mornings.

The men would be packing themselves into the Cadillac; I

could hear their voices and see them from the upstairs window as I dragged my bones out of bed to get up and go flush the toilet. I could see out there in the driveway my brother sinking back down into the back seat and settling his boots up flat against one of the rear windows, hear the engine starting, hear, I think, "Mack the Knife" playing on the radio, and it was like this that the men left the farm in the mornings all that summer before our house was built, while our house was just a hole in the ground. They left spewing loose gravel from underneath the Cadillac tires, probably scaring frogs out of the drainpipe sections along where the driveway met the highway, where they would take a hard left to get out on the road, passing along the row of Burma Shave signs in the Cadillac, passing them by, flying the Confederate glory like starting flags.

After crossing the bridge over into K.C., they would thump a bumper dragging left down on the old road down by the river flats where, whirling dust, our dad would be driving along and lifting his hand up off the steering wheel or tapping his horn at the drivers going the other way, drivers driving trucks of all sizes with his name stenciled on the sides, our dad all the while running organizational plans and ways to secure debt and flavor-combination ideas by Winn, and Winn, his whole body pitched about by the car ride, Winn, not my brother, would be listening as our dad drove the three of them deep into the industrial section of town to where his ice-cream plant was tucked behind the gargantuan Empire Cold Storage Company.

Once, hay mower in the distance, sun a bright butter curl on the lustrous butter plate of the midday Midwestern sky, two men from the plant arrived out at the farm with Winn—he was old and he got tired—and also bringing along with them an

institutional-sized and industrial-quality top-opening freezer
case with three double lift-up black rubber lids to plug in on
the kitchen porch. They were carrying it up the yard toward
the porch, the very porch where I would usually be lying on
the old tasseled sofa that was moved there from where Winn's
hospital bed now was, our dad having changed the furniture
around for Winn's special needs—rented the hospital bed,
hired on some help, bought the BarcaLounger, moved the
tasseled sofa out to where I would lie in a loose Hawaiian shirt
I found in the cedar closet left over from the story about when
our dad made Winn go on that Hawaiian cruise, forced him
to leave the state of Missouri and fly all the way to Honolulu
and get on a cruise boat. I wore that shirt all that summer for
its comfort, switching off from my Memphis peasant blouse. I
even sometimes slept in it at night, and in the hot afternoons
after the freezer arrived, me in the Hawaiian shirt lying on the
tasseled sofa, I could reach over my hand to the institutional
freezer for, say, another ice-cream sandwich as I was reading
my comic books or drawing and being lulled slowly but surely
into our new life here in the North by the sleepy ironing-board
creak of "our help," Roberta, the fine churchwoman who was
coming to Winn for a few hours each day, who hummed
whiney church songs as she ironed Winn's shirts, her ironing
board set up in the afternoons between the BarcaLounger and
the picture window while Winn would lie in his hospital bed
moving his lips along with whatever Roberta was singing.

From time to time, dropping a foot on the floor and elevat-
ing my old bones upright to a full standing position to see
better what kinds of novelty items there were in our new
freezer, I would go on into the kitchen and drop down at the
kitchen table next to our mom, who would be sitting there
having a cigarette and some of the iced Constant Comment tea
everybody had started drinking in Memphis, her pockets wad-

ded with Kleenexes, and soothing herself with doing her bad habit she never could break: she would be fidgeting and peeling at her fingernails until they peeled off in layers.

So we sat while the dishwasher chugged and threw the dishes around inside, her with her fingernails and sipping her tea and smoking her cigarette, and me eating, perhaps, a Cho Cho cup with a little wooden spoon, and together we would stare into the parlor at Roberta ironing, watch to find out when it was that Roberta made those iron-shaped scorch marks on Winn's shirts. It was when the car pools came and caused a big honking ruckus in the dancing-school parking lot across the highway.

Even my hostile brother and, most especially, our grinning energetic dad would smell good and manly whenever they came home to call it a day, to seek out some plain old R. and R., their clothes and hair and skin dusted over with powdered milk and cane sugar and chocolate-mix powder, plus dirt and sweat, and bringing along with them cartons of new ice-cream items that they had thrown in the back of the Cadillac and brought home packed on dry ice. They were ready to eat chicken-fried steak, pot roast, or chicken, chicken, chicken— that is, if they were home anytime close to a dinner hour, since our dad worked everything. He worked production alongside his crews, all the shifts our dad worked in the course of a week since they kept the plant running around the clock in the summers for the obvious reasons. And also he did figures and answered phones in the front office right along with the clerical ladies, his fingers virtuoso on the keys of the adding machine processing orders and tallying inventory and doing the payroll. He might slip into one of the quilted freezer-room jackets that were kept hanging on pegs and two-handed pull open the bank vault of a freezer door and disappear into the thick spill of arctic air before the door slammed shut behind him.

And then he might be coming around the back to the loading dock to load up the trucks, and he was not beyond jumping into the cab of a truck to make the deliveries himself, even driving those great big trailer jobbies, the ones with sixteen gears and a copilot, driving them down to Chillicothe. He was always going places like Chillicothe back then.

It was the things that did not sell that he brought home to stock our freezer with as much as the good stuff. Such as he would bring home eggnog ice cream in half-gallon cartons and Coconut Xmas Snowballs with the real little wax candles sticking up out of the middle of a holly-berry bunch toothpicked in the top. He'd bring pumpkin-flavored turkeys and green dye #11 Christmas trees. At the plant, there were bags of green dye #11. Roberta would serve more bowls of eggnog ice cream than any other flavor to Winn and my mom and me at noontime with our cold-cut sandwiches. We never saw from her hand an Eskimo pie or a Drumstick. The vanilla-and-pumpkin-flavored turkeys she would serve occasionally. The strawberry Valentine hearts once in a while—but it was something about the eggnog ice cream that had Roberta in thrall.

There were times in the evenings that summer when I would have to go the long way around to get from my room to the kitchen, where my mom would be starting our dinner, maybe grating carrots for our little salads or peeling potatoes, it being too early for her to start on me about my job—pouring the milks for dinner. I would have to go through the dark dining room, slip past the set of sliding oak doors of the parlor where I could hear our dad and my brother in there, with

Winn asleep or watching the action in his hospital bed, our dad always sitting in the BarcaLounger and my brother always sitting in the needlepointed armchair with the arm doilies. Basically what it was was our dad loving my brother so much he could not leave him alone, so afraid was he for my brother concerning life and wanting everything for him to be so proud and good and strong, for him to be strong and good, and my brother just wanting to be left alone to have some one or two of his own experiences just for himself all by himself, to be proud and good and strong and good just all by himself without our dad acting as brilliant, genius interpreter to every little thing, every little time he brushed his teeth, and Winn sometimes even sleeping, who knows how, through those two saying, "Why do you think why?" to each other, or "Just what do you mean by that?"

Or "Is that what you think life is?" It could be either one of them saying that.

"What do you think life is? Tell me right now, please, your theories on what life is?"

My brother would finally somehow get himself excused, and then he would head outside past the floured chicken parts frying up in the iron skillet and the others waiting their turn on a waxed-paper sheet, past the finished pieces draining on paper towels on the countertop, past the Jell-O mold quivering in our mom's hands as she was maybe walking it over to the refrigerator, past me and the institutional freezer with the black rubber lift-up tops. He would maybe yell something at me, seeing me reading a comic book on the tasseled sofa, "Taylor, you lazy imbecile, go get the dandelion digger," and then he would go on out into the downy evening light to pull out the old rusty push mower from the shed. I would watch him from where I would climb up on the freezer to watch, and I saw him more than once that summer drop down on his knees in some grass beside the push mower to examine something on the mower blades or wheels, some little thing, a mud clot or something dried up and stuck up there in the mower, and my brother would just get down there close next to it and poke it with a stick.

Our dad would stand beside me and watch. "What in the Sam Hill?" he would breathe while he watched my brother doodle around with the stick. Then our dad would follow out, not really being able to stay away from my brother, and he would go off across the yard the opposite way from my brother like he could not watch anymore but still so my brother could see him, like maybe he was going on back to work. He would back his Cadillac out of the barn, back it right underneath my brother's Confederate flag. Then at this point our mom would run out in the yard and our dad would hit the brakes and pretty soon he would cut the engine and come on back in the house, going back past me again, me with my bare foot rummaging around in one of the pull-up top openings of the freezer, and he would go on in to sit with Winn, where they would together look at the TV evening news or do figures or just wait for the chicken to finally get itself fried.

Then one night, early on, us all lying out in the sweet-smelling just-mown grass my brother was made to mow by our dad, we all were lying out after supper having our dessert ice-cream bars in some ratty lawn chairs I found stuck up in the rafters of the barn I had been crawling around in that day while trying to hang out of the hayloft and fix the corner of our Confederate flag where it had come loose. We all were much interested in Cremesicles at that time—vanilla ice cream on a stick covered over with an orange sherbert—something our dad was giving a try that hit BIG, and still is BIG, as you probably know if you frequent the freezer case at the 7-Eleven, but what you would not know is it was my dad that made it that way. We were eating the first Cremesicles on the planet Earth and looking around us like you do, and we could see Winn watching TV and eating a Cremesicle too, lit up in the picture window in his hospital bed. We could see him perfectly, like it looks when you are in the dark outside and somebody is on the inside with all the lights flipped on and funny just because they *are* so totally unawares. The TV noise was blaring far louder out there in the crystalline country air than it would have seemed to be if we were, say, back in the city of Memphis and standing in front of the Peabody Hotel waiting for our car to be brought around front and this same TV noise was blaring out from one of the upstairs hotel windows.

And with us each shifting our bones around in our wooden lawn chairs, we could see the back of a billboard the Motel-6 motel chain, headquartered around there somewhere, had up there, with electric lights haloing out from around the dark oblong of its back side since it was set forwards for the oncoming traffic to see, not our way. The Burma Shave signs we could not see, but there was the perky spotlit dancer on top of the dance studio across the highway outfitted with her top hat and cane, and actually it was she and Winn that outshone by far even the Motel-6 or the Confederate flag that was nailed up on the barn and lit up ghostlike from all the night neon and from our pride—my brother's and mine. Though that was a shame; the Confederate flag was by far the most beautiful and really meant something important too. It meant the human spirit and causes.

Our family conversations were mostly round-and-rounds

where one person would get going on some topic dear to their heart and then one other person or persons would have to get him off that topic ASAP because it was becoming a threat to one or more of the other family members' equilibrium. And then another party would launch off with a topic that soon could not be tolerated by one or more of the others. And around and around it went like that with conversations in our family.

Our mom would say (I know this since this is what she said all that summer), "Houses are never done on time," and our dad would let her run on for a while to get that off her chest, then he would change the subject because what could he do about the house anyway, build it himself? He would change the topic to something like "work"—his work in particular or just "work" in general—and my brother would pretty soon launch into the Civil War and start talking about a battle or a summit even more obscure than the one he talked about the night before since that is what he was talking about all that summer. He might as well have been in the Civil War for all he knew about it. Or he was also saying every other sentence, such as when our mom was going on about the house never being ready, "Let's go back, let's don't do this," and our dad would get us off that topic lickety-split by launching into something like what he said the night I am remembering.

He said, "Oh, family, this place has a history. Oh, this place right here and that old man up there in that picture window really have a history. It scares me to think if it weren't for this place and that man."

And how could we not, even my brother, how could we not look up at the picture window and see Winn, who, at this point, was holding his Cremesicle stick in his mouth and drooping it down like I saw the French apache dancers do with their cigarettes on TV, and my brother then said, "What is that he is wearing? Is he wearing my T-shirt? Is that my T-shirt?" and I remember I jumped up on my feet in order to get a better look at Winn.

Our dad then could have said, for example, to get us off that topic, I don't remember exactly but this is close, "Taylor-tater-tot? Do you know how to snap the head off a snake? Winn in there does," which is probably the thing that started my mom down the road I am going to tell about now, because our mom did say one of those drive-in movie perfecto nights, one of those early nights while we were probably all still trip-rattled, which is maybe why this thing she told had such a BIG impact on me, why I sucked it up like a damp sponge being wiped across an old kitchen counter, our mom said, "You all? Oh, I heard this story. Oh, I just heard the most horrible story from home in a letter. Something so sad. Something so terrible."

"Don't tell us," I yelled out at her, attuned as I was to her different tones of storytelling voices, as I was getting myself back in my lawn chair from trying but not succeeding in seeing Winn's shirtfront. "Don't tell us," I yelled out, wanting but not wanting, I didn't really think, to know her story—all this I had decided just from her tone.

"Snakes reminded me," our mom said.

"Oh boy. Hold your horses right there just a minute," our dad said, working at getting himself up out of his low rickety lawn chair, getting up and then going in the back kitchen door, where we could see him stick his head in the electrified parlor where Winn was, then disappear, then come back and toss something in Winn's lap. Then our dad came back out and threw us underhanded, one after the other, a round of spoons and each our own Coconut Xmas Snowball.

"Here's yours, here's yours, here's yours," he said. "Come on. We got to eat these up before they get freezer burn."

"Well, okay," our mom said, as flakes of coconut were drifting down into her lap from the split she had made in the cellophane wrapper with her teeth. I got out dad's Zippo and went around lighting the little candles on everybody's Snowball, staving off the story since I did not need a new story. I had plenty of other stories stored up to get hysterical about. I did not need any more right then. There was the move story, which we were living, so it was not yet really a story; it was our life. There were the kitten drownings. There were penises. I had not yet reconciled myself to penises. There was the mule.

"Well, okay. Here I go," our mom said, gazing into her tiny dancing candle flame. "You know Pete and Jenny Rogers and their little girl from the Cotillion, don't you, honey?" she said to our dad. "And it was the Cylinders, the Richard Cylinders, not his brother Benjamin, not the one that you know. John Cylinder married to Linelle, and Patience, her niece, was on the swim team with you, Taylor, at the country club. Peter was a year behind you in Scouts, son. They were the ones that lent them their cabin over by Pittick Place, down on Hamlin's Road by South Tar Creek. Not Arkansas and not Mississippi."

"What in the Sam Hill are you talking about?" our dad said—just barely ever was he able to tolerate the way our mom went about telling a story—but not daring to shift us off the topic altogether by bringing up the further adventures of Winn or something, as she had her rights, such as to tell an occasional story.

I was working hard on my granite-hard Snowball, also letting the candle drip wax on my fingers as I chipped off little bites.

My brother was staring over at our mom, interested in spite of however she was going to get the story out.

"Okay," our mom said, inhaling a deep breath of honeysuckled air and clearing the decks by setting her Snowball down to melt in the grass by her lawn chair. "I'll try again. There were young newlyweds, the young Pearson couple you all remember from Memphis that were getting married even before we left? Mary Rogers. Mary Rogers Pearson. You saw her picture, Taylor, in the society a few weeks back. Remember? I showed you? Well, they were lent a brand-new cabin for their honeymoon up in the Smokies—and it was the first night right after their wedding party, and, you know, they were very tired, so they got in bed . . ."

Here my ears pricked up like the mule's must have done when he saw Uncle Winn walk over to the woodpile and reach down his bare arm.

"On the bed I hear there was one of those chenille bedspreads with the peacock," our mom said, lighting up a cigarette just then, finally relaxing a little into her story, finally having gotten a couple of sentences out unimpeded by the rest of us. The smoke hazed over my way, where I smoked it in through my nose.

Now this story our mom was about to tell I have repeated many times. Over the course of my girlhood, I have told this story, I think, whenever I have spent the night with any one of my many girlfriends, also boyfriends, men, and husbands later, now that I am grown. But this version I am writing here is the most permanent record there has ever been of this story.

Well, the honeymoon couple, Mary Rogers Pearson and her husband, got in bed (sex, penis), and they soon heard things moving around on the floor—slithering noises (snake)—and the husband (penis) said to his beloved, Mary Rogers Pearson, he said that he "must take a small break, my darling, so stay just like that in the bed for just a moment" so he could go and see what was causing those noises (snakes slithering plus rattles being dragged across the floor) before he continued on with what tender, gentle bliss (penis) he was bringing to his bride for the first time in all her life, and as he hit the floor with his feet and began to feel along the wall for a light switch, he was right then stepping on top of rattlesnake on top of rattlesnake on top of rattlesnake. It was a whole nest of them he was stepping on! Some damn idiot fool had had the stupidity to build that cabin right over the site of the biggest nest of diamondbacks in the whole state of Tennessee! And those snakes were tangled up everywhere! And the noise level! But the young husband was a Southern boy and thought only of his bride, Mary Rogers Pearson—which it would behoove me to be like her, however she was, so I could find someone to think of *me* like that, so our mom's look said to me, our mom with her cigarette smoke ribboning into the natural plus neon-lit sky—and though the young husband never made it to the light switch in that dolt's cabin (there was a lawsuit), what with those rattlesnakes striking and striking at him as they would of course do, them being wild animals, and him stomping all over them barefooted like a grape stomper, he screamed out to Mary Rogers Pearson, "Oh! my darling! For God's sakes! My love! Stay in the bed! Oh, my darling!" as he was, by that time, simply sacrificing himself for her because he could have instead, if you think about it, screamed for her to go and get him some help. But he didn't. He said to her, "My love. Don't move a muscle! Don't move! Don't even breathe! Just stay in bed! Just please, for Christ's sake, stay still in the bed!"

And then he was quiet. And the rattlesnakes eventually began calming down, almost all of them.

And Mary Rogers Pearson, beautiful, luminous Mary, huddled up on the bed, her bare shoulders marbled in the wedding-night moonlight that streamed down across those Smoky Mountains and poured on in through the cabin window. Mary Rogers Pearson, who was armed only with her honeymoon nightgown of Italian lace, which was bought for her in Memphis at the Helen Shop, Mary did fine. Mary held on and did fine.

Now our mom's cigarette tip brightened considerably as she took a deep drag, and we all sat quietly for a while, each alone with our own thoughts.

"She bowed at the Christmas Cotillion," our mom said.

"And they had their wedding reception at the country club," she said.

"The minute we left Memphis this all happened. The minute we left or the day after," our mom said.

Oh!

Oh!

Hearing the sounds she had to have heard! Knowing what she must have known, maybe even seen because probably she could see shapes and shadows and even more. I mean *really* SEE.

Oh!

I could not imagine that much, being big enough for that much TERROR. And in the morning—as our mom was telling it to us, us glommed on to her every word by now, us at her complete mercy—there was the poor dead husband with too many rattlesnake bites to even count, his WHOLE body a mass of bites, the rattlesnakes by now all gone back down to their nests underneath the floorboards of that cabin like they had never even been there at all. No one really saw them come and no one saw them leave except for what Mary Rogers Pearson said she could see.

"Did that really happen?" I said, wanting my drawing book, my fingers itching to get around a pencil. "Did that happen? Who told you that? When did that happen?" I said, struggling underneath the crushing weight of this story.

Now the mule and mule-type stories that were so rampant back then—plus there were others I haven't even mentioned (such as the "wild dog" shootings, dogs people did not want anymore, dogs people brought out from Kansas City and let go out on the road by the farm)—maybe, maybe, maybe I could just barely tolerate life knowing those stories happened in the same world I did and that living things had felt what I had the unique genius to imagine in minute detail that they felt from what I was being told had happened to them, and maybe the violence of us being Rebels forced to live here in the North with the Yankees, that too I could make a semblance of peace with if given a little time, but this story with the honeymoon and the snakes coming up in the dark from underneath and no way out but by getting in with the snakes, and Mary Rogers Pearson in her lace nightgown from the Helen Shop—that story pushed me over the edge because I was never one who could make peace with things by saying what seemed to take care of everything for everybody else, which was Oh well, that's just the way it goes. That's life for you. *C'est la vie.*

"It happened," our mom said, glancing down at her fingernails. "You see, listen to me, Taylor!" she said as I was busy balling up my Coconut Xmas Snowball wrapper and struggling out of my chair.

"Taylor-tot!" our dad said, meaning he knew I was sealing over and they were not done with me yet.

"The bride," our mom said, "Mary Rogers Pearson, she stayed right there in the bed and she kept still," our mom said, facing me with eyes as glittery with purpose and adamancy as our dad's were when he was driving us up here from our happy home down in the South.

"She did not allow herself to lose control," our dad piped in. "She kept *still*. And that was smart. That was her only way out of this mess. And well, how she did it, Taylor, if you are wondering just how she did it—well how she did it was how anybody does anything, how I do what I do at work. She *had* to, that's how she did it."

"That's life for you. I swan," our mom said.

"I saw Winn do a rattlesnake," our dad said. "Winn just

grabbed him up by its rattler and cracked it like a whip. Head popped off. Then Winn kept cracking until he had cracked him off into nice little wiener-sized sections for the buzzards."

We all gazed up at Winn's picture window and there was Winn sitting straight up in his hospital bed peering back out the window at us. And he *was* wearing my brother's T-shirt. It was the one with the Confederate flag.

"She's okay," our mom said. "Mary Rogers Pearson is doing pretty good now. Went to a Fourth of July brunch at the country club."

Now. I could see no path from that night and those snakes to being anything like "pretty good." None whatsoever. The only path I could make out was the path where I would start screaming my head off and all the snakes would charge up and jump all over me—or maybe, maybe I could make it through the night by accident, by being frozen by fear or something or by some survival mechanism just built into the species that I did not even know I had, but that would be only to be carted off to the insane asylum the next morning where I would spend all the rest of my life reliving the snake-night honeymoon from the razor-sharp picture screen buried deep in my head.

In the late afternoons at a certain time, I would go and lie down on the wood floor under my brother's bed to wait for him to come back from his day of work at the ice-cream factory. If I had the time right, my brother would stumble in and flop down in his big rubber work boots on top of where I was stowed, and I could hear him up there talking conversations to himself about things he would be thinking about and remembering and trying hard to figure out. He would lie still on the bed and sigh loud enough so I could hear his breath swoosh out. He had not yet really begun to unpack his heart from his over-and-done-with life he used to have back in Memphis, where he would do things like take the bus crosstown with his friends and go to the movies.

I was younger and my heart maybe unpacked quicker.

My brother would get up off the bed and kick his boots off and go into the bathroom and get himself a glass of water. Then he would come back and lie down and breathe and sigh some more. Sometimes he would get off the bed and ramble down to the kitchen to get a loaf of Wonder bread, his afternoon food of choice, and sometimes he would trap me by coming back in our room at the wrong time, such as when I was half in and half out from under his bed.

Lots of times when I was lying under his bed, I would find down there beside me a loaf or two of older, forgotten Wonder breads. I would lie down there and, like he did, pull the crust off slices, then ball up the soft middle part to make bread dough, and I found I liked eating it that way as much as he was liking it up above me. For the most part, I was sympathetic and together with my brother in most ways, but he never knew it or cared. Back then, there was a time that I would have been him if I could.

Like our dad, I had quit sleeping. Like our dad, our mom's sleep method was too hard for me. I could not bear the idea of boring myself any more than I already was bored.

During the day, I found two-by-fours nailed to an oak tree I could climb up in and take my drawing book. I began drawing, along with all the usuals you already know about, I drew that cabin in the Smokies and Mary Rogers Pearson in bed with her young husband. I drew the rattlesnakes snarled and snaked around under the floorboards. I drew one of the snakes peeping up through a little knothole in the floor. Then I would look through the tree leaves and draw the silhouette of the dancer in a top hat and cane on the top of the dance studio across the highway. I drew our good old Confederate flag nailed up on the barn, the billboards and Burma Shave signs, the waving fields of grain and the puffy clouds, the cars that shot by out on the highway. I drew where the mule used to be, where the kittens were drowned as fast as they could get themselves born—and I would draw these things as my brother was pushing the mower around in the grass below me, learning more about the meaning of the word "work."

When I climbed higher in the oak tree, I could see farther out to where the subdivision with our new house was going in, to where the municipal airport was, to where there were turnpikes and interstates all crimped together with toll-booths—the "I-this" and the "I-that," the "I," I suppose, that had brought us here from the South.

I started taking walks. For something to do, I'd lumber down the old cracking highway that went by in front of the farm, and I would go toward the future, toward our subdivision with the special fancy entrance gate and brand-new sod and the new flagpole that was flying a regular flag. I would walk along the flat curved streets to where our building site was located, where I would watch the men pour cement for the foundation, where I got to know the carpenters framing out the rooms, where I would mess around in the wood scraps with some glue, a hammer, and some nails. I would walk around on the springy plywood floors and in and out of the framed-out rooms—walk around in the space where my parents said my room would be. Then after a while, I would leave there and go and explore the other subdivisions farther down the high-way that had names such as Dundee Hills, Edgewood, Glen Briar, Green Briar, Briarcliff, and Briarcliff Manor. Briarcliff Manor sat on a bluff overlooking the waterworks and the turnpike and the municipal airport. Way off in the distance, you could see downtown K.C. and smell the stockyards.

At night I would go in by our sleeping mom's bed and drop down on my knees beside her pillow and whisper, "Mom, Mom, Mom. I can't sleep. I can't get any sleep." Then I would sit and wait, maybe get a glass of water from the bathroom, and I would wait and study her. Watch her for how she did it.

Then one night was the last; after that one night where nothing different had happened, I never came in her room that same way again.

She could sleep. I could not.

Things happened. A small plane fell out of the sky and crashed nose-first into the open roof of a half-built split-level. I ran and saw the perfect undamaged tail of the plane sticking up higher than the walls, and there was a wing I walked up and down on lying off with some rolled-up sod.

A farmhouse burned down to the ground—ancient electrical wiring—and our mom, Roberta, and I heard the sirens and all of us came running out of the kitchen, ran across the highway and on back behind the dance studio, where we watched as fire trucks jammed up a pasture and boys dragged soggy, sooty mattresses and grimy sofas out into the yard, as a boiling fire took that dried-wood house all the way down to the ground. Then below the ground.

There were other wonders. Rains that would snare-drum on the tin roof of the kitchen porch with the sun out, shining and hot. Also heavy, weighty rains that would flood the low spots in the yard, sopping rains where I could run out and dance myself around right across from the dance studio, then flop down by a ditch and let clear water run over my stretched-out legs, let rainwater paste my peasant blouse to my chest and back and shoulders, to turn it see-through, to fine, thin Italian lace, and I would, feeling myself "her," lift my chin up and stick my chest out and just sit there being—beautiful.

Our dad and me, we were both of us up at night. If Winn were not so old, he would have lasted all night with us, but as it was, Winn was pretty much a transistor radio pulling a weak signal from a long way off and real, real late at night. It was simple old age that saved Winn from that torture you need to be young like our dad and me, young and strong, to take. Anybody else would just collapse. And in the day, if you don't sleep at night, I found you cannot let down either. The whole problem is you cannot let down ever, so you must be able to work up a great jitteriness to get you going up and over your exhaustion in the mornings and to keep up with a kind of wasp-attacking-frenzy energy throughout the day. Though I was still occasionally glancing in through our mom's door to see her sleep, and our dad did in fact stick real close by Winn in the BarcaLounger even though Winn was often asleep himself and not great company, our dad and I kept pretty much quiet with each other and everybody else about our nights. We would just include within us more and more of this problem, which became like any other thing we could not do a darn thing about. We were on our own, each of us alone, like I was beginning to think we all were anyway.

I would be coming out of my bedroom and pad on down the hall under a sweeping wedding veil of drifted cigarette smoke that collected into a swirled wasp-nest motif around the overhead light fixture (with the wasps asleep), and when I had made my way down the steep stairs to the parlor, there would be our dad, beanbag ashtray on knee, sitting in the Barca-Lounger next to Winn's bed in the quiet of that old farmhouse where all you could hear was the refrigerator and our institutional freezer and the whole house that turned over from time to time in its deep sleep. He would be dressed in his flight suit from the war and would be spooning ice cream out of a mixing bowl, scowling at numbers and figures that were listed out on a big tablet of paper.

At dawn I would finally just get dressed and go on out of the house swinging my arms, turning cartwheels, going up and down the tree several times to get the blood going. I would slide under a forsythia bush for a heartfelt prayer (so what) that never changed one thing, never made the slightest difference other than, unlike our mom, I was let down every time I tried it.

So carrying along on the side of the highway heading up toward our building site in the morning-milk-splashing-on-a-bowl-of-cornflakes sun, in the day-camp-bus-picking-up-the-little-kids-with-their-lunch-sacks sunshine, I would find Bic pens and No. 2 pencils and plastic barrettes lying along the side of the road. That is not true. That was only sometimes. Mostly I would find sticks and broken pop bottles and all kinds of wild flowering weeds, which I would pick, the weeds, sometimes having to get down on my hands and knees and bite off the stalks with my teeth if twisting and turning and picking at them with my fingernails or sawing at them with a broken Coke bottle did not work.

I would see up ahead in the roadside debris a glint or flash, and I would walk faster; then I would see it was maybe only the inside wrapper from somebody's cigarettes causing the sun to flash, or the even thinner foil liner of a Nestlé's Crunch bar. Once in a while it was the foil cover of an Eskimo Pie bar with our dad's name in small letters under the logo. Once it was a fifty-cent piece that bought me a small packet of something for my hair at the highway Rexall where I had been in seeing what all they had. It smelled like vinegar when I mixed it with water, and when I rinsed it through my hair after washing, my hair shined so it was me who was the one causing the sun to flash.

In his big floaty Cadillac, our dad, with Winn and my brother packed inside, would sometimes come surging down the highway passing me by on those mornings. Sometimes I would jump up and down and wave my bunch of flowery weeds at them or throw a stick out in the road. Once I tried to kill them all by aiming a Coke bottle at their windshield. Another time, though, our dad slowed and crunched over onto the shoulder of the highway close to where I was standing, and as I went up to his side of the car, he made the most charming talk to me. He said, "And how are you, Mademoiselle Taylor?" and he said this in the French manner he learned from when he was in France having R. and R. from bombing the Germans, and I remember clear as day that "Mack the Knife" was playing on the Cadillac car radio and that our dad and Winn were together and smiling and happy.

No. *Really* happy. *Really, really* happy. They were the heart of happiness; but us two, my brother and I, we were the skin or the coating or something.

I had myself slung out along a tree branch looking down on top of my brother—I could see his head and the tops of his T-shirted shoulders shoving the push mower up and down the slopes of the yard, his arm reaching down from time to time to throw a stick or a rock out of the way, then hitching himself up again and shoving off to mow more grass—and I was thinking about how I would never want to be mowing the grass and that obviously neither would my brother.

Our mom, who is in charge of me, I just wait out. I stay in

the tree. Like the milk. Pouring the milk at dinner. Pouring milk for dinner is my job.

So slung on the branch overlooking my brother pushing the mower in rusty-blade-rotating shoves, I was busying myself with picking around and collecting acorns and small branches, things to drop down on his head as he would shove under my tree, things to ping off his flag-shirted shoulders, as I listened to him say, "Why? Why? Tell me why. Why is this such a big deal? I would just like to know."

He was out across the yard in the dandelions and I could see the wheel nut fell off again or the mower was jammed up with a stick again. He tried getting it going by assuming different positions—like one foot braced up on the mower for extra push force and then the other foot up on the mower and his shoulder braced on the handle, or picking up the entire mower and turning it over upside down, saying, "Why, why, why?" I watched him through a kaleidoscope of oak leaves as I was changing around my position in the tree, going from one side of the tree to the other, the arms flapping on my Hawaiian shirt, my hair hopefully flashing in the sun, and then I noticed him coming stolidly up the little slope, passing right under my tree, where I froze on my branch and took aim and bombed down on him a couple of the acorns. He headed into the garage, where there are the tools.

Asking for more, my brother walked back under my tree (more acorns, twigs, some spit) and on back down a ways to the push mower, where he kneeled and dropped his ass low in the dandelions. "Get me a Bomb Pop, Taylor," he said over his shoulder. "Get out of the stupid tree and go get me a Bomb Pop, or a Popsicle is okay."

I held still in the tree, flattened on my branch, my hair with the great drugstore stuff hanging down to where even I could see the different growing-out lengths, to where the glossy ends thinned to a translucence from the woven sunlight that was worked in through the leaves.

My brother pulled off his Confederate flag T-shirt. He pulled it over his head and used it to wipe across his face, then glancing up at the bigger Confederate flag nailed on the barn, he worked at tying his shirt up around his head so it would flop down his back, flag out. Turning, he looked up at me.

I flattened flatter.

"Popsicle, Taylor," he said. "Or I will come up there and kill you."

Grasses rustled from the little suppertime breeze. I was about ready to just go and get it for him, to get him his Bomb Pop or Popsicle. The sun, I noticed, was an egg yolk drooped over the fields as I shifted around on my branch, then monkeyed over to another branch, the back of my Hawaiian shirt floating out behind me. My brother was watching me and saying, "Go get me a Bomb Pop, *now*, Taylor."

Then it was what I think must be sleep, that I was dreaming, the automatic reaction of, say, Mary Rogers Pearson happening in me; I froze. I was so quiet beside that delicate slipping through, a delicate slipping through is what it was, that I must have been sound asleep (finally) and dreaming this thing, this moving stillness up there beside me, which after a brief pause set off my shoulders to press back, my rib cage to part wide for air, my lungs to grab for reaches of sound that I grabbed hold of, dug my heels in, and wrenched from my heart. Arm on its own volition reached out and grabbed hold of the moving stillness, and we fell, the two of us together, moving stillness now a garden hose with the water turned on full (but no water), we fell tangled around in the Hawaiian shirt that flew up around my neck, we fell through the air together to land on my back out of the tree to there where my brother was standing with us rolling around, me screaming out, the garden hose all muscle now with trying to get away, undulating, coiling, and wrapping on me, my shoulders pressing forward, legs trying to stand up.

I got hold of, not the tail, but the whole rear third and unwound it off my body. Up in the air my arm went and straight up it went, but nothing. Nothing. So I did this, pretty calm too, I held it in one hand and found a better grip with the other, and then I did it, I cracked it again, but all that happened was it looped. It sketched a U shape in the air, so I did it again and let her fly, or he got away, or he got himself, herself, up in the air, where she gave a bronco lunge and charcoaled several W's and landed a ways off deep in the dandelions over by where my brother was standing by the push mower. He, she, swished through the grasses, or she—she—went back to her babies. Or she *was* a baby and her mother was a mule-eating Missouri-wheat-crop python waiting out there in the field for me when I went looking.

The picture window was a crowd of faces looking out, Winn in the middle sitting bolt upright in his hospital bed.

I fixed my shirt down from around my neck and went up the yard to get my brother his Bomb Pop. I got a couple of Bomb Pops out of the institutional freezer, our mom and dad calling out my name from the parlor, and then I ran back outside to my brother before the sun dropped its yolk completely into the field and the day was all over. We sat down together, my brother and I, by the push mower, my brother in his lawn-mowing misery and me welling with snake force and power, and we tore the wrappers off our Bomb Pops.

No one is in charge of me.

Hot

I will get older and wear wool suits and count on myself and the baby will ride around Wall Street on a motorcycle. But for now, here is how it barely is—enough things to sit on my soul and bring me down to a soft whirring, to stop my hair from whipping and slapping me in the face—some things, not myself, to count on.

Sweet darling, I am hot by morning when the sun edges the drawn shade with gold and I wake to the clacking and the chimes. There are dried, stiff fish skeletons you might comb your hair with layered out there, out my window, layered like bananas in a bunch on palm tree trunks, and they are what I hear clacking most like plastic in these dry days. There are wind chimes out there too, mixing in, and the fellows downstairs run their dryer mornings, I can smell their softener gusting up here, and it is a comfort.

For now, it is all too beautiful sometimes with me having so much wide-grinning time, a desert of time, a triple feature of time—time it takes courage to have.

I rub my finger, wet it first and rub it along the ledge, moving slow, bulldozing stuff up into a little hill, shaping it, squaring the corners with my fingernail, working to get it right. I know when it is right.

With their long leaves, those trees paddle the air, slapping and grating themselves up along my screen, grating their raggedy ends clear through, and snowing down into the other side into my room, screen-powdered to dust, lying along the ledge.

I write "my little baby" in the dust. He is bucking on the floor, his diapers barely hooked on his hipbones, the floor probably no cleaner than the ledge, and I take hours for anything, hours for anything, with breaks only for food, for bath, for naps—but I have all day most days, me up on the bed eating candies I keep hidden, maybe under my pillow so the baby will not know. I take care to keep the papers quiet, him up here with me or on the floor on his little woven blanket and me sneaking a piece of walnut fudge I buy on our walks. These days will not go on forever.

There is a house being built. Sawing out there, which is a nice thing, a nice sound, though I admit I need the wind chimes, would never be without them now that I know what they are about. You should get some and hang them on a porch. No, don't—I might give you some—oh God, and listen to this, here is the thing: in bed in the dark. That, and then me in the middle of all these things, my favorite things outside and in here. I love slipping my body down along the sheets themselves. One that I know, there is one who knows me and tells me things, me in a moonlight that turns us sand-colored slick with sweat, our ribs rippled dunes, the moon squinting at us from behind that aforementioned fish-boned tree out there projecting jungle patterns neck to thigh. What comes is all the reasons anyone would ever want or could ask, for waltzing on with this life.

I leave the baby with Rosa days that I have to, and I leave him at the ritzy church when there is a ladies' luncheon, a function for me to weasel my way out in the world from. I kiss him goodbye on his cheek—he is my moon child, I could eat him with a spoon, eat him with a spoon, and I leave him safe in the church ladies' good care. I leave him finally, regretfully, dragging my netted soul out the door and away, like when he screams in the night and I have nothing else in me that I can see to do for him—which breaks my heart. And it is at those times I find I have to shut the door and go on and do something else.

Trembling with freedom, I tear my nametag off, seek out shadows, glide along walls, hug myself up in the carved stone alcoves of this church that smells sweet with simple chicken salad and warm breads, those Parker House rolls, like the gusty dryer downstairs—and chicken salad, or did I say that?—and something else, something in the wood or in the hymnbooks, something they light and burn. I slide out the back way into a bucket of afternoon stars dumped over my head, goofy now (it's that freedom), and do a pratfall for old Will sitting out there after he has done the cooking but before he does the dishes. There is Will settled nicely into loud daylight—which, like flashbulbs in the face, is painful, would be even for an old-time movie queen, ta-dah.

Will can be counted on to smile. He smiles and wears one funny shoe for his poor hurt foot that—I do not know why, but it never heals—is an open sore. Something tending the yard. I kneel in front of him, I bow my head, I do not know why I do this either, but I want to see, and I slip the open shoe off his foot and pick up the folded gauze.

Does not bother me in the least. It has nothing to do with me, me who fingers wet with saliva trace the curve of waist, slipping along over this body with the crazy trees out the window and the music of the wind chimes and the little baby bucking up on his knees in his crib, little fat knees to chest, in one movement grabbing up his bottle and rolling over on his back, and the other, slipping me up onto him, pulling me up onto him by holding me and tugging under my arms.

I sit side by side with Will on the bench I move him to, him hobbling along close beside me, the bench in a softly shaded archway with the vines and climbing roses weaving through as, my loose skirt slipping low between my legs, I comb my hair out from where I have it twisted up, high and wound around with a patterned scarf. Then I twist it back up again off my neck, just the same way I had it before.

Will puts one splayed hand on my knee pushing up, and he says, "Miss, you too young for this place," which always makes me cry for some reason whenever anyone says that to me, and I stop with my hair and tip my face so sun splashes glancing off my cheek, and I let him move his hand, and for a while I do not flinch.

I cross the street, then another street, and then wander down winding like a vine where things get stylish—to my husband's office, where I look up and find his mirrored windows. He said he saw me once down there on the sidewalk, he said, with a soft Santa Ana stirring my hair so some strands stuck to my lips, and the ends, he said, they danced up like flames.

Sometimes I keep going down the street to try on narrow dresses or to look for shoes with straps across the instep that buckle or to sip Cokes with lime slices and ask for crusty lemon sole with slivered almonds at his little brick building of a town club, me sitting off alone in the dark-paneled dining room.

And sometimes I go into the building where he has his office, and I ride up in the elevator to his floor and walk down past his gold-lettered door straight to the office across the hall, not my husband's office but another office where there are receptionists safely corralled off, walls of files, doors somewhere that open quietly, then close quietly. And bouncy music, that grocery store music, that dentist office music, lively yet muted. There is, too, the sound of butcher-block paper tearing off a roll in the back. I look around and find myself a seat with the others, and like them I look at magazines or stare at the fish tank or look up at the people occasionally walking by outside in the hall.

Of course he sees me, he knows me, and almost with a ballet step, he turns a quarter turn, his hair longer and slightly saw-toothing over his collar as he tilts his head and muffles his smile. Now, of us women who wait, I have been the quietest one, the littlest mouse sitting in the big leather chairs, and he says my name before I begin to rise up on my feet never looking at the others, never knowing if they know he has taken me out of turn, and I follow him back through his little maze of halls, out the back door, down to the underground garage where his car is parked, not far from the church where my baby is with the church ladies, and we get in the back, and he reaches up my skirt, and he pulls my panties down or sometimes just moves the crotch aside with his hand, and I help him, I hold it there for him to the side—he is not a magician—as I lie back on leather seats that smell like leather.

I wander alone the streets of this place. It is afternoon quiet, hushed before rush hour, and I know I have to get my baby early before the other luncheon ladies come for their babies and questions are raised.

The church babysitting lady is so kind and my baby happy and clean. I take him to the park. He is awake and ready, and we sit off alone near a fountain of water that falls like ropes, and to the sight of this I nurse him, the milk ready in me for him—and I nurse him.

From where we sit, I know I could see the windows of my husband's office and next to them the other's office if I looked. I do not know what the wife my husband had before me did to him that made him leave her, and now me, to make him leave me, but now I do know, baby, no matter what it was, sweet baby, I would do it too.

The baby tugs at my breast and works his face into a frown, he works so hard at this nursing. He is so small, his back square and flat. It fits the palm of my hand, though everywhere else he is round but his back. It makes me straighten my back up with him as I sit and look out at the cars going by. And the cars, they seem to pull the asphalt up in strings, it is that hot.

Graceland

Because I got out is the reason life picks up when I fly in and that I bring along some Yankee—it makes them wild, stirs them up. But this time, flying in, something in the air means things more, and it is not just my Yankee is worse than the others I have brought along with me at other times. No, I think it is death itself adding the somber note. I felt it reaching its hand up to my airplane as my airplane was glinting in for the touchdown. It was a finger I saw outside my window seat crooking down, and I pointed it out to Bradley, who said he could make it out too once I had shown him what I felt.

It is true that only because I am in town Agnes cuts into her crucial praying time and gets up off her knees and stands herself a little taller even though she is sick and is hot and clammy and some other thing the tests have shown that have got her crazy scared, and she is standing next to me dressed in fuschia chiffon—and this is how I know it is me that is the reason for these changes, as she is touching me and no one else, weaving her fingers with mine, drumming her nails in my palm, kissing me on the lips and behind the ear. Bradley stays close, is rocking back on his heels, lowering his chin, and seeing out from prescription sunglasses that get light inside and dark outside, and is looking over at the mural on the wall done in greens—of Spanish moss and a plantation.

Agnes is wondering about him, and my guess is so is everybody else wondering, and she says to me, "He looks like an Italian count, and you look different too, Justine," she says. I will not discuss me, but I do take the time to tell her no, that Bradley just looks like he looks because he works in a big department store in the men's department and gets a discount, is where he buys these wonderful clothes he wears that probably are from Italy, in fact they probably are, I am sure of it. And she nods and twists a ring I am wearing on my finger—it is one of the ones she has sent me in the mail, and I look over at Bradley, and him tall and thin, and I see where Agnes is getting her thinking from, from nowhere other than just from looking with her eyes like any one of us could do.

Me, I will not get into with her and discuss. Agnes has her ideas of how I should look to look my best and this is not it, since I have lately done myself up in mostly black, starting with a black little skinny dress, my hair color now changed to black and my hair ratted out full away from my face—but my lips red as berries is the look I have now, all my own new look except for one thing; I am wearing a lot of big chunky jewelry, all of it what she has been sending me in the mail, all of it hers—like pearls and aquamarine earrings and thick gold-chain bracelets and more; there is a giant flower brooch pinned on my dress. I have thought to bring her a present though I do not know when I can find some quiet for her to open it.

We all are waiting a long time to move from the cocktail

hour to the big table for dinner because we all are tied up with waiting for certain cousins to arrive from where they are driving in from the eastern part of the state and they are not too reliable.

But Agnes is, to my mind, becoming more reliable the way she sees things. Clear as day she sees things. More than just seeing Bradley and noticing my change in dressing style, Agnes sees things close to the way I do, I have recently come to know, as we have been writing these letters back and forth since things got even harder in my life, with me trying to find someplace to make a life on this planet and her finding out she was soon going to be leaving the planet altogether.

We started out with dashing off little notes and cards back and forth and her saying she had gone to the doctor before or after her bridge game or ladies' church luncheon and me saying, "Oh, I know how scared you must be because I got back this bad smear from my doctor back here in the East and I am worried half to death," and then her saying, "Come on home, Justine, and let us take care of you," and her sending me a bracelet or some cash in the mail and me writing back and saying, "Don't worry, Agnes, I had another one and it all went away, it cleared up, I think it was the carrot juice Bradley fixed me that did it," and her writing that there is a shadow on her X ray and me saying, "Agnes, you come East where the real doctors are that will know what to do about that shadow," and her saying no, she would die on the airplane and finally her writing me in a different tone altogether and asking me about did I know what happened after you died and me writing her back the things I think about that as best I could, me writing her back plainly because she is clearly desperate with wanting to know from somebody and her saying in so many words she has never been so alone, and so I say I know I would be scared like her, if I was like her, if I was ninety-one years old and sick, and I tell her just that in my letters. I tell her to keep praying, that I would, you bet your life, that I know I would be at Lourdes right now if it was me. And I would be, too. I would be in Mexico swallowing apricot pits if it came to that, I would be rubbing bat grease in my hair if it would help, I would be hysterical like her, out of my head. And so she has been sending me her jewelry and even some large bills in the mail to my little apartment, my little place, and her letters are getting more bald with the truth of her heart with every one I get, and so are mine starting to be with the power of telling the truth as we see it to each other, and it is a dazzling experience, the most dazzling of my life to now, I tell you, Agnes and I discovering each other.

They circle around us, blood family does, holding drinks. My Yankee turns from the mural to the window and his glasses are graceful, they darken up spreading like dye in water just because he has turned toward a lamp. There is no sun in here.

"Well, I want to speak," Agnes says, "before the cousins get here even. I just want you all to know that I am glad you are here, and as I told you already, I would rather see you all together once more with me alive than for you to come back to my funeral where I would not know it."

Then somebody says, "What in the Sam Hill funeral are you talking about, Agnes?"

"What funeral, Agnes? You are looking grand, just grand," somebody else says.

"Let us drink a toast to Agnes," a third person says, and everybody is raising his glass and drinking to Agnes, and she looks over at me, and I look over at Bradley who has got his shades that are black now up on his head with tufts of hair sticking out from behind the earpieces, and it is at this time that the French doors fling back, and it is the cousins, Foster and Tapper, blowing in from the eastern part of the state late, just arriving.

There are a lot of Hey, y'all's, How you doing's, and Foster and Tapper, in tandem, head to the bar laughing and elbowing each other and talking about how they need a jump start for this old party. Agnes comes over by me and says for me to be nice to them, Justine, so I say I will, and the next thing I know we are seated at the table, and Bradley is down at the head with Agnes, and I am at the other end between Fos and Tap.

"Like your little bitty skirt, Justine," Foster says. He is big, with dark hair. "I like women half naked," he says.

I tell them about the East and ramble on about how I am doing with looking for a job.

Then Tapper, who is quieter, with tight lips and blond wavy hair, thumbs down the table, referring to Bradley, and what he means is where in the hell did I get him, and Foster says, "Just what is it he is wearing anyway, some kind of tweedy faggy ensemble or what?"

This sets them off laughing, and next they upend their drinks and have to do rock, paper, scissors to see who is going to the bar for refills.

I say to Tapper, "I read about you all in *Time* magazine."

Tapper waves Foster back from the bar, yelling across the dining room, "Get over here, Bub. Justine's brought up the World's Fair."

They say, boy, they wish that World's Fair would come back, as there are the lawsuits and they could use the money. They say, "I mean, Justine, that World's Fair was some godsend, I never had so much fun as when that thing was going on," and they both are speaking now, one says one thing and the other one says the next.

"We got this tram concession," Foster says.

"Had those little trams with the awnings," Tapper says.

"We got an exclusive," Foster says.

"And we let the people park free in our 7-Eleven lot," Tapper says, and they went on like that.

"And then we charged them ten dollars to go back and forth on our tram," one of them says.

"Why didn't you all come down, Justine, and have some fun?" the other one says.

Then Tapper gets up and goes and gets three more drinks for us, and the dinner keeps on like that, and my stomach is rumbling, and I am hungry, and all I have had is some little tiny Cajun things off a tray a waiter has passed.

I look down the table to where Agnes is sitting and giving me concern and to where Bradley is since he is the person who I have brought along so I will be able to wink at him and have him excuse himself and come and talk to me is the plan, maybe put his arm around me and act possessive for five minutes or go and get me another drink or maybe even this, tell me, just say to me, Justine, you must stop now, you have had enough to drink and drinking more will not help one thing and I am taking you and tucking you in bed back at the motel out near the airport so we will be ready for our flight out in the morning.

But Bradley is having fun now, or maybe I never made his part of the plan clear, and I see he is pushing back his chair and doing something with his napkin like snapping it out in front of him, and I see Agnes, see that her head is kind of slumping over like she is looking at something in her lap, at least that is what I hope she is doing. Her hair looks a little off-center, and that startles me it is so sad and so pathetic, and I feel tiny needles of panic fire off in my upper arms. I think that I have not done a thing for her yet except wear her jewelry and spend her money on plane tickets for Bradley and me, and I am worried that I will not think of anything to do, that I have done it all by just writing her a few letters, and I know, I know it has not been enough, oh no, not enough, not what I am wanting.

Now Foster and Tapper are shut up about the World's Fair and are watching Bradley too.

"Now what is that dumb Yankee doing now, Justine?" they are saying on either side of me, and I see Agnes's head is dropping even lower than before.

There is nowhere safe to look, it all upsets me, every bit of it, so I am looking out the window of the dining room where we are, and I can see snowball bushes heaping up, which bring like a formula to mind Agnes's jewelry I am heaped all over with, and parked beside them is maybe what I think it is, my mind does a thing, there cannot be too many of them around. Looking out the window of the private dining room and next to a pink snowball bush is—heavy with metal, holes, big tires, and old—Agnes's car, her old Oldsmobile. No matter how old it gets it is her new car to me, and new-car smell is triggered off in my head until I am not imagining, I am smelling it like it really is.

"Earth to Justine," Tapper says.

"Now, look at that dumb Yankee," Foster says, and my head snaps around off the car, and I see Bradley is doing origami with his napkin, I swear he is. He is making certain folds with the corner, then laying the whole napkin out on the table and doing a couple of crosswise folds across the middle, then holding it up, bending it all around. The ladies are leaning forward, and even the help is lined up behind his chair watching, and he holds it up about eye level, and all of a sudden we all see Bradley has made a dog out of that napkin, even with a little tail on it and floppy ears, and he is tossing it one-handed across the table where there is a scuffle to catch it, and then all the women clap their hands and say, "Bravo, Bradley," but not Foster and not Tapper and not me and not Agnes.

I am trying to think of a way to get Bradley to look at me, as it is time for the motel even if I have not given Agnes her present yet—I can mail it to her—but that is not to be, as then he starts in again on someone else's napkin, and I recognize the folds—he is going to make an airplane and will throw it down to our end of the table, I know, and he will probably hit me in the head with it, messing my hair, Bradley will.

"You want to see something, Justine?" Tapper says, jerking his chair closer to mine. "You watch Foster here. Do it for her, Fos. Hang on, Justine. You just wait, Justine."

Foster grabs up his napkin in his fist. "I am not going to make some wimpy dachshund, uh-uh," he is saying, and he starts folding his napkin, keeping it deep in his lap the whole time while Bradley did different, Bradley had his right up there where everyone could see it the whole time, but Foster is doing different.

I start thinking about myself and about Agnes, and I start thinking one thing: that she may be dying but also that if I do not get myself out of here I will be dying right along with her, or before her even, and not have lived sixty of the years that she has on her, I will just have skipped right over them without a trace and be dead before she is. We are in an even race it feels like, and both of us are going flat out.

Foster says, "Now look here, Justine," and he is making more folds in his lap, and Tapper has his arm resting on the back of my chair and is crowding me, and I am watching Foster's lap, and slowly it rises up, a long white napkin point coming slowly up out of his lap, and he says, "There, Justine. Now what do you think of them potatoes? This here is no dachshund."

That is it, that is all I need. With or without Bradley I am pushing back my chair, knocking into a waiter holding a rack of lamb, and I am going on down the table and grabbing Agnes up out of her chair and draping her over my arm—they all think I am taking her to the ladies' room, even Bradley reaches a hand back at me as I walk past his chair and he pats in my direction—and Agnes and I head out some French doors onto the flagstone patio, and we tiptoe through some clipped grass in our high heels, step over the parking-lot stones going to the waiting Oldsmobile, Agnes's car, which is not locked and which Agnes has the set of keys to. I say to her, "You are sick, aren't you?" and she says, "I am sick to death, Justine, but I do not want to go home or to the hospital. Maybe I will want to go later, but not now."

I get her settled in the front seat and go on around to get in the driver's side but not without picking a big heavy bunch of snowball flowers from the snowball bush. All colors I get mixed up in the bouquet, and I lay them down on the seat between us. The front seat is like a love seat or a small couch, and the seat belts just strap across our laps and buckle in the old way.

As I start up the Olds, the engine sounds like it has phlegm in its throat, nothing like any new-car sounds, nothing at all, and I find a big two-lane avenue by the country club with big mansions on each side and get us going down it so Agnes can talk to me about anything, and we have all night is how I see it, as I am not leaving here until the morning. She does not mind the wind blowing her hair, she says, and anyway, I go slow, I have just nowhere to go in a hurry at all, and we roll along, her reaching over to put a stray piece of my black hair back up where it goes, and I reach the back of my hand up to her forehead, then to her cheek to check for a fever, which she has, that I know, and then she does it, she does the thing, she reaches up and instead of straightening her hair she takes it off and drops it on the seat beside the flowers between the two of us, and when I look over at her, I see she does have some, just a little bit is all, just thin wisps of it in long thin strands here and there on her head.

"Well, I do not know where to go," Agnes says, "but I want to go somewhere and just sit with you, Justine."

And I say, "Agnes, I have not lived here in a while, but I will try and find us someplace for that."

I think to go and get us a bite, but neither of us wants to eat or go anywhere where there are people we might have to say something to so I just ride us around, Agnes taking off something from time to time, like her watch, and strapping it on my wrist, and then her ring and slipping it on one of my bare fingers, and next she is taking money from her purse and stuffing it in the side pocket of my purse, and nothing can get her to stop doing these things.

After a long while driving I get an idea, so I turn the car around and head us in the other direction, as now I know where it is that we should be; I head us way over across town through stoplights, and when I tell Agnes where we are going, she says, "Well, Elvis was always kind to his mother," and I guess he was at that, always kind to his mother.

We are at Graceland and Graceland is closed, so Agnes and I just sit out in the Olds in front of the locked gates, which is as close as we can get ourselves to all that that Graceland is, and we wonder to each other for a while if Elvis is dead or not—there is always that rumor—while a guard saunters around from time to time to check things. Then it comes to me to do something. I grab up the snowball bouquet and slip out of the car and go up close to the fence to see up at the house, but it is hard to see anything much in the dark and there are no lights. My arm with the fewest bracelets is the one I work through the fence bars reaching for some blades of grass from the lawn to have something, and those bracelets Agnes gave me clanking on the metal bars, metal on metal, waking the dead, and this tickles me for some reason, me loaded down with things *I* would not be caught dead in, stealing grass blades at Elvis's, and Bradley back at the country club stuck with my relatives, and Agnes as close to being spirit as possible and now in my sole care, Agnes looking on. I pull some blades of grass up by the roots, then, standing up, decide to give the snowball bouquet a heave right over the fence there, and with Agnes watching me, I do just that, and the snowball flowers arc up in the sky for a minute and that is the end of them that I can see.

I get back in beside Agnes, and I drop a few little grass blades in her hand, her taking them in her fingers and messing with them as I am digging out the present I have brought her, out from my purse, Agnes saying over and over, "Honey, I do not want anything from you."

She tears the paper and drops the ribbon on top of her wig, and she has my present—in a silver frame, a shot of me, shot so my eyes stand out bleached and lined with black, how I am doing my eyes these days. She says to me, after staring at my picture for a while, she says, "Justine, I do not care what you do or how you get yourself up or what you try next," and I am feeling one of the heaviest loads I had been carrying lifting off my heart.

I start the engine just for the heat now for her, she is shivering, and I say to her, "Agnes, you keep on with your program, Agnes. You are not just anyone to let go and slide down in the mud, you have not lived ninety-one years to do that with yourself."

Then she scares me to death. She says, "Something else, Justine," her breathing in my ear. "Something else, Justine."

I look at her, holding her but holding her back from me a little, and she says, "I am so scared, I am still scared, and I cannot believe it that I would feel this way by now but I do. It is not any better going into someplace you just do not know, you do not know and cannot see."

I say to her, I say, making a mistake saying it too, I now think, I say, "Agnes, you are making me scared with the way you talk about what is ahead because I would expect by now you *would* know and that you would be at a kind of peace by now."

Then Agnes starts messing with the grass blades, her hands kind of jerking, and I am more scared than before because I think maybe I just told her to shut up is what she is hearing from me or that I told her in so many words she *should* be peaceful, old as she is, and I see next she is putting a piece of that grass between her lips to try something I cannot believe she would know how to do, but she tries to play something on that grass blade, but all she can do is make buzzings and sharp twerps, and mostly it sounds like air rattling through her lips with no grass blade there at all, and I am wanting her to stop but do not know how to say that to Agnes, so I put the Olds in reverse and back us carefully into the boulevard there in front of Graceland.

I drive us around town like that, Agnes playing never anything really but noises, though once I think maybe I can hear something. After a while I see Agnes drops the grass blades in her lap, just lets them scatter, then she curls her hand softly over some of them and turns, looking at me.

So I say to her, now driving down the boulevard with the mansions on either side, I say to her that we have to go on now, Agnes, and I head us back across the town.

Solace

First thing was, when he got himself together, he called up the boys. They hadn't gone anywhere. They were at the same row of barstools that they had always been at, so all they had to do was unhook their toes and drop their feet down off the rungs and slip onto the floor and walk over and pick up the dangling phone with C.W. breathing all over into the other end of it. The gist of what was said between them was "Where you been? We thought maybe you fell in."

Next thing, it became on a regular basis a thing of C.W. to go down to town, bouncing down the hill to the bar from his mother Iris's house in Iris's station wagon with his elbow jutting out the window and with his trumpet in its case sitting up there next to him riding shotgun. With his free hand, C.W. would be swatting at all the dogs fighting to keep upright behind the wire-mesh partition in the back, those dogs he'd been dreaming of and had got hold of so easy. He had found them mostly just trotting in the spindly weeds by the side of the road, or one old one he had caught up with zigzagging around the back of the Stardust Country Club, where some weekends C.W. was playing big-band dance music with the boys. Another dog he had come across in the parking lot behind a root-beer stand. This dog was acting skittish and shy, so C.W. had had to coax the fellow to him by kneeling down in the gravel, grubbing up his tux pants while making himself alluring by offering a plain cheeseburger in his get-on-over-here hand. Anyway, C.W. had named these dogs Stardust, 7-Eleven, Route 57, A & W, and so forth, which were what-ever he could think of for names.

Back home at his own mother Iris's house was the only place C.W. could think of to go and live and lay his head down (and be fed okay), so this is how come his abandoned wife, going along on her way to the grocery store, and his deserted son, rattling by inside the school bus, could often see C.W. out front of Iris's—him and Iris together, sitting up on the front porch, holding lite brews, C.W.'s feet balancing up on his upended horn case. They would be together soaking up the low-level buzz of the cicadas crawling out of their bug holes and assem-bling up along the bark of the big elm trees about that time of day, while C.W.'s pack of dogs would be tearing around acting like maniacs, sometimes stopping to lick salt off the tips of his fingers and even sometimes getting his arms wet all up and down, you know, his arms.

Next came women—sometimes several at once.

C.W. could even get younger and younger ones thrown in with the older ones. Sometimes the older ones looked as good as the younger ones—but still, C.W. liked best listing off the ages of the young ones to anybody he could get to sit still for five minutes and listen. Even his nice enough abandoned wife he did this to once, but only once.

At the bar, late one night, with his dogs asleep everywhere

around the gravelly bar entrance and with one woman goofing around standing behind him, her arms looped loose around his waist, the front of her knees poking into the back of his knees, and—get this—a second woman standing in front of him leaning back and resting herself onto his open-shirted chest—C.W. gets to thinking about his teenaged son, the dark and depressing though academically strong Eugene.

"Here's what it is, Eugene," C.W. says, phoning Eugene up where Eugene is already up all night standing in front of his closet mirror with his horn, getting to be the next Don Palladino, the all-competent, studio lead trumpet player from L.A.

"Here's what it is, man," C.W. says to Eugene.

" 'Man'? You're calling me 'man'?" Eugene says, hyperventilating from it being his dad on the other end of the line.

"Yes, man, I am. Here's what it is. Your daddy can't fight it anymore what he's doing, even though nobody, including him, don't exactly like it . . . yet I do like it, if you know what I mean."

"Yeah," Eugene says, numb-lipped from hours of grinding away doing his Schlossberg, his scales, his intervals, his Arban, his Herbert L. Clarke études—all this to build tone and technique. Hanging on to the phone, he slides down the wall so he sits on the floor, his extra-long spine he inherited from his mother curving into a soft fluid S shape. He gazes at himself in the closet full-length mirror and then flattens his nose onto the glass and tries breathing that way for a while.

"I'm happy, man! I'm happy," C.W. says. "What do you think of that?"

"Okay," Eugene says, waiting patiently as he hears the sound of the phone clattering to the floor, then the sound of it being picked back up.

"Son? You there? Listen. I'm happy. I'm really having a time," C.W. says.

"Okay," Eugene says.

"I got me some dogs," C.W. says. "I'm following my bliss. You know about that?"

"I guess . . ." Eugene says.

"I love you, son. I love you, man. I just love you, Eugene, and I want you to know that, and so—well, dude, that's all she wrote!"

"Oh, boy," Eugene says.

"Say, son," C.W. continues, shrieking above some new crashing bar noise. "I got an idea! I'll take you on an away-from-home gig with me. Me and the boys—we got this road gig!"

"I'll pass," Eugene mumbles, fogging the mirror.

"No, man. No passes. This happiness bus is leaving with you on it. No siree bobcat! On this trip there are no passes allowed."

Trip morning dawns.

Eugene is pacing the side yard holding his horn over by his grandma Iris's bee-jammed zinnia bed where Iris used to like to get on her knees in the dirt clods and crawl around among the muskmelons and smoke Camels—back before the dogs.

C.W. is one big walking talking grin he is so full of himself and high on life, hitching his pants up and pushing his aviator shades back up on his nose and striding around Iris's yard from the house to the car and back from the car to the house loading luggage and horn cases into the trunk of his brand-new gig car, this one bought to last, a solid French Peugeot, solid like a truck—a thing he has been waxing on and wiping on until the streetlights are liquid splashes on its surface in the gentle evenings after supper.

Iris, worrying a mole on her elbow, watches from the front

porch with the dogs rolling and twisting on their backs in the dewy grass and gathering in a pack to chase under the front tires of speeders gunning by.

Two women who don't look much different one from the other—they look skinny, yet full somehow—drive up in a car with rusted, thinned-out places around the wheels and an empty baby seat showing in the back. C.W., with his mouth kind of twisted and talking to be funny out of one side, says, "Where you been, ladies? We was thinking maybe you fell in, weren't we, Eugene?"

The women climb out of their car, smoothing out the rumples in their shorts, and with their fists, they pound the dogs on the dogs' flat heads to get their snouts out from wedging in their crotches, and next, while the dogs are circling around, snorting and regrouping, the women grab C.W. back around where his neck hairs are bristly, at the same time knocking his aviators cockeyed so that they hang and swing loose on only one of his ears. C.W. gives the women both big bear hugs in the middle of the front yard, dramatically ending with bending them, one off each arm, over backwards into full-blown professional acrobatic backbends, their shiny crimped hair drifting out from the back of their heads and softly unpleating through hard-ass sunlight.

When they return upright again, the women laugh and squeal and say, "What is with these dogs!"

"Well, I got smart dogs," C.W. says and sneaks a look over at Eugene, who is flatfooting it around in the zinnia bed in his leather oxfords.

The women notice Eugene too. "Weren't you in high school?" they say.

"Still am," Eugene answers.

"Well, these ladies aren't," C.W. leaps in and says. "This is Renee, and this here is Donna. They are divorcées, grown-up women with kids and alimony and everything—aren't you, ladies?"

"Well, only little babies," Donna says, retying her halter top up around her neck so that it fits her better. "We got ourselves a couple of babies, so that part's true."

"Any you guys want any pop or anything?" says Renee. "We got an ice chest in our trunk we're bringing along for the trip."

Popping the pop-tops off of five cream sodas, one after the other, and handing them around, Renee and Donna clamber up on the porch to introduce themselves to Iris, who is up there busying herself with rearranging wicker porch furniture and blowing thoughtful curlicues of smoke from the Camel she is smoking.

"Must be nice having C.W. home," Renee says, wiping off a chair with an extra-damp dishrag Iris has gone and gotten from the kitchen.

"His hours are a little irregular," Iris answers, waggling her eyebrows for expression and speaking in a monotone.

"Hmmmmmmmmmm—" the women say, and they all circle around chairs to sit in and light up Camels, then start confessing in the same plain way as Iris—in a monotone, waggling their eyebrows just from seeing her waggling her eyebrows, woman-to-woman—about how hard a job mothering can be and how *glad* they are to be getting out of town, even if just for a few days, much as they *love* their babies—and also for the blessed chance to flop down beside a swimming pool or sit in front of a TV set ALONE.

The three of them get somber for a moment. They puff seriously on more of Iris's Camels and sip the last of their cream sodas and steady-gaze at Eugene, netted in gnats over in the zinnia bed, bobbing and weaving insanely while blowing on his trumpet. He is practicing the first section of the new piece he is working on, "The Carnival of Venice."

After a while, Iris finally gears herself up and stands up out of her chair and yells over at Eugene. "Come on out of the flowers, Eugene," she says.

"Eugene?" C.W. says, slamming down the trunk of the French Peugeot. "Son? It's too hot for that right now. None of us can hear."

Renee, raising her voice to be heard over where Eugene is now working the same few isolated bars over and over again, messing up at the same place each time, Renee says, "You know, Iris? I'm already feeling tired. I would just as soon stay right here on this peaceful porch, to tell the honest truth—just let them go on the gig trip without me, much as I like having a good time as much as the next person."

"The more I think about it," Renee continues, her crimped hair bringing to Iris's mind the roof of her toolshed out back, "you know, Iris, we could play cards and treat ourselves to dinner out."

"We could sit out here and read magazines, couldn't we, Iris?" Donna chimes in. "Like C.W. does, and think a straight, simple, uninterrupted thought."

"I don't ever really get a chance to just flop, do you, Iris?" Renee says.

Iris blows another long, thoughtful roiling curlicue of smoke, little wrinkles sunbursting out from around her lips, her rock-steady eyes set on a point on the horizon past which the dogs have organized themselves into a unit and are chasing a swerving laundry truck up the street. After a while she says, "Well, I wouldn't be going on that trip, not for all the tea in China."

"Iris, you don't have a phony bone in your body," Donna exclaims. "I hope I'm like you when I'm your age."

Iris, not ever really looking at them, draws deep on her Camel and lifts up her eyebrows.

Meanwhile, tagging down the street behind his pack of dogs,

C.W. screams out, "A & W! Stardust! Stardust! Stop it, you dogs! Get back here, you dingbats."

"You see that, Mom?" C.W. yells back at the porch. "If I can get Stardust, I got them all. Stardust's made himself top dog!"

Iris and the women shake their heads.

Eugene, who has pretty much worked out the correct tonguing in the first section of "The Carnival of Venice," is now starting the whole thing smoothly over from the very beginning.

"Eugene! Can it, man!" C.W. yells, hunched over with his back and knees bent, coming back down the street dragging by the collar a growling Stardust, whose four legs are locked at every bendable joint. Eugene stops for a moment, looking like he is wavering between playing some more or knocking off altogether.

Iris speaks. "No, girls, I prefer to stay right here to do my worrying where I can see what's going on. As you can see, I need to be braced for it at all times."

"Let's go, ladies!" C.W. says. "Your chariot awaits you. Dogs, give me a kiss. You be good for Grandma, okay, dogs? No tearing each other apart. No sex either. We all love you, Grandma, you hear? We love you."

Eugene looks across at Iris where she is standing up now on the front porch waving goodbye to the women and holding her cigarette out a little bit behind her, flicking ashes through the side-porch railings. The little dog there's talk of calling Chili Dog is leaping up on her legs, tearing snags and making runners in her stockings.

Watching his dad hanging his tux shirt on the special hook in the back seat of the French Peugeot and the women getting their stuff organized so they can get at it if they need to during the trip, Eugene is struck by the way C.W. is now a regular guy with girlfriends and a diving watch and aviator shades and styled, funny-combed hair that sweeps long pieces across his head and dogs and a car he messes around with in the driveway in the evenings after supper. He even has a mom he dumps his shit on—just like everybody else.

"He's real fast, isn't he?" C.W. says, whizzing down the hill, strapping the fancy seat belt over him in several places and running up the windows and punching the air-con buttons, then moving the slide to HIGH COOL all at the same time with the kind of ease that comes only from being a total expert at what you are doing.

The women are turned around in their seats watching out the back window. Stardust, his tongue flipped back over his shoulder and kiting out almost serenely, is giving it his best shot, running with his paws rifling madly through the air.

"When we outrun him, he'll go back, so don't you worry, any of you," C.W. says, moving on to the next thing. "Now, this here French Peugeot is the greatest, huh, isn't it, ladies? Man, I always wanted me one of these things. The day I saw this baby sitting there on the foreign import car lot, it said to me, '*Venez ici.*' "

C.W. turns the jazz station on low, and talking in that funny voice of his out of the side of his mouth, he says, "So! You ladies getting into this or what?" Then he scat-sings "da, ba, da, ba, da, ba, do, be, do, be, do" along with the cool, complicated small-group jazz he hears things in nobody else does, except maybe Eugene—who's beginning to have an ear. Eugene—who's no lightweight, who's beginning to know what's great, what's good, and what's just a pile.

The air smells fruity and sweet from the women, it smells spicy from C.W.'s hairspray, and from Eugene it smells from his own cotton shirt from where he picked it up off the floor in the back of his closet at home—it smells mostly like his own condensed self, like his own skin, his own hair without any added stuff. The women slouch like rag dolls to show how relaxed they are getting to be, their breasts lolling and rolling on their rib cages in their halter tops and dropping looser and lower with each passed mile. They exhale deep soulful breaths and say, "No babies! We don't have those babies crawling all over us. Whooo-weee! What a relief."

"No babies!"

"Whew-weee," C.W. says. "No dogs. Whew-weee."

Eugene upends his cream soda and studies what he can see of C.W.'s reflection in the oblong of the rearview mirror. There is nothing much to see—only C.W.'s black sunglass eyes, his longish curly sideburns that appear and disappear as he moves his head with the music or when looking over his shoulder to pass cars or talk to the women or occasionally to say something back at Eugene sitting in the back seat.

"What do you think of your old dad now, Eugene?" C.W. says, noticing him.

"About what?" Eugene says, his mouth and sinuses foggy and sweet with cream-soda fumes. Then, pretending—even wishing—Eugene digs his horn mouthpiece out of his pocket, hunches over, and starts blowing through it, blowing it like a duck call, imitating the way the women sound to him with their talk about their babies and about hanging out at the bar and about when lunchtime is coming up.

"Hey, Eugene," C.W. says after a while, punching up the sound on the radio to get him to stop doing that thing with the horn mouthpiece. "Listen to this, man. This is IT—the THING itself. Note here the genius of the all-time top dude—Stan Kenton! Stan, I love you, man."

Renee, readjusting something that's poking her in the waistband of her shorts, murmurs, "I like Herb Alpert. You guys know Herb Alpert?"

C.W. drops his hands in his lap and lets the French Peugeot drive itself. He thinks about what to say or do. He exhales a low breath. They pass through a tollbooth. "Renee," he finally says, "you should be put out on this road for that."

"How come?" she says, sneezing and making Eugene immediately see one of those special sneezes on TV where the virus germs roil and tidal-wave dust-mote-style around in the churning air of the car. "He plays the trumpet too," she says, grabbing on to Eugene's arm to get warm.

"It's cold in here," Donna says from the front seat.

"Put on a sweater," C.W. says. "Eugene? Son, find them sweaters. Look through my stuff back there on the floor. There's sweaters."

Without budging a muscle, Eugene says, "There's no sweater." Renee sneezes again and clings on to Eugene, wedging her hands deep into his armpits.

"Don't wipe your hands on me," he says in a snarly way at her.

"Trade places then," she says, starting to get mad. "C.W., look—Eugene's on the sun side. I'm the one getting sick stuck over here on the cold side."

"And we have babies back home," Donna says in the front seat.

"You're all right, Renee, aren't you? We'll be stopping soon and then you can sit wherever you want. Hell, we'll all trade around. Mix ourselves all up," C.W. says.

"But it feels to me like every single one of the blower things is aimed on my neck and arms and shoulders. I can even feel it on my legs," Renee says.

"Oh, fuck," C.W. says. "Fuck the whole air-conditioning system, man," he says as he smashes his fingers over all the window buttons at once, so all four windows hum down, the warning flasher goes on, as does the dashboard map-reading light.

With the windows open, and with the sun and wind gulping in, the women's crimped hair flags and snaps with single lit strands sticking to their lip gloss. C.W.'s hair is danced around, with one long, much longer, hank of hair being lifted up off the top of his head to streamer out behind. Eugene, ankles together, knees dropped, slobs his tongue out and pinches the women's long hairs out of his mouth and then he lays them, one by one, wet across Renee's naked knees or up arcing over Donna's bony shoulders. In the front, C.W.'s eventually cheerful again, off and telling long, convoluted, involved, rambling, detailed stories about his dogs and keeping busy with thinking up some good names for the dogs that are sure to turn up in the future.

"Let me know if you see any," he says, while his ruffly tux shirt, hanging in the back seat on a wire hanger, puffs up gently, all soft and billowy—then, flat, cracks back and forth with arms slapping.

When they stop for a fill-up, bathroom, walk-around, and lunch break, Eugene starts the self-serve gas pumping, decodes the raising-of-the-hood secret, then leans his upper body way in under the hood, his long body elongating out of his pants enough to reveal the beginning of his butt crack. He swabs the oil thing in the oil hole. He nudges some colored wires and floats his hand over several hot pieces of metal, then glances over at the wild-haired women heading off across the asphalt, walking with their elbows pumping their feet along, one of them in white flip-flops, the other one clomping in tooled cowboy boots, both with droopy cloth purses slung off their shoulders, and them heading toward a rinky-dink tourist trap.

"We're going to go look around in there, okay? See what's in there," Renee yells back over her shoulder.

"We'll be right back, okay, C.W.?" Donna says.

Coming out of the gas station and walking fast himself around back of the cinder-block building, C.W. waves them off while twirling a key on a big wooden paddle. He booms in a big, deep bandleader voice, "Ladies, you go on. I'm going to go see an Indian about a blanket."

"Don't fall in," Donna yells.

"Don't worry. I won't be sitting down," C.W. shouts out before disappearing out of sight around the corner.

Eugene tightens some screw-on things in the engine, then wipes his hands on a paper towel and slams down the hood. He tucks his T-shirt back down tight into his jeans and rambles around for a while checking out the various gas prices marked on the pumps. He gives in to the urge to dig his trumpet case out from under all the stuff piled in the car trunk and then slouches over next to a Coke machine, where he feeds in dimes, one on top of the other. After a few delicious pulls on a bottle of RC, liberal with thin lacy ice chips polka-dotted all through it, and with the sunshine draping a pleasant enough warmth on the tops of his shoulders and no one irritating him particularly at that moment, Eugene stands up ramrod straight, takes a deep breath, and hits from nothing a high C sharp and then actually hangs on to the sucker. After another pull on the RC and a couple of deep diaphragmatic breaths, Eugene drops down a couple of octaves and plays a chromatic C-sharp scale, inching up note by note with an even and stunning perfection. Even C.W., from what he is doing at the moment, holds his muscles rigid and listens with an alert, artist-to-artist, and not exactly unpaternal, intensity.

"I got a present for you," one of the women singsongs, clomping up behind Eugene and messing around with his pants, pulling and tugging, trying to wedge something into one of his back pants pockets. Eugene jumps a little, then lowers his horn, carefully laying it on a spread-out paper towel on top of the Coke machine. He does a spin, kind of Oriental, his hands rising out in front of him, and he grabs the woman—it is Donna—by the arm, yanking up.

Donna starts fighting him back by screaming and grabbing on his fingers, getting one isolated from the others and trying to bend it back.

Eugene squats down and jerks himself free. He gets a new grip and wraps Donna up around the waist with his arms so she can't move. He starts hitting her on her head using the timeless technique of hitting her on her own head with her own hand and saying as many times as he can get in above her yells, "Why are you hitting on yourself? Why are you doing that to yourself. I'm not doing anything to you. You are doing it to yourself."

Renee, unawares, doodling with her earrings, comes slapping around the corner in her flip-flops, having to stop from time to time to shove her foot back in where she has flipped one clear off, and when she sees what is going on between Donna and Eugene, she rushes over to help out Donna by patting and fumbling Eugene all over, searching him for loose, unfisted fingers.

C.W., trundling back around the corner from the john, where he has also been on the pay phone to Iris hearing all about home—Stardust was hit by some hot-rodder, A & W made a mess in the dining room, Airport's wandered off—C.W. sees Eugene and the women. He sees Eugene staggering one way and then the other way loaded down with Renee clinging on his back while he is stomping all over her little slipped-off flip-flop that's half buried in the gravel, grinding on purpose thick black marks all over the new bought-for-the-trip white rubber.

"Finish it up!" C.W. screams. "Finish it up!" C.W. says, grabbing Renee around the waist and unhooking her various holds, one by one, off of Eugene. Then, while draping her across one of his hips so she's out of the way, he screams directly into Eugene's face, "Eugene? You done now? You need more time, son? I can give you more time. Not much, but some time I got."

"It was a Snickers bar," Donna says to Eugene. "I got you a Snickers bar, to be nice."

Then Renee says, "Hey, Herb Alpert. Look at that, Herb Alpert. You let this pathetic little squashed-up Snickers bar get you all bent out of shape?"

"Get out of here!" Eugene screams, the tendons on his neck standing out, his jaw jutted. All the while C.W. is trying to steer him, after much arm jerking away and fierce eyeball confrontation, into the rest-stop restaurant and to get him situated far out of the way, over in the back, deep behind the salad bar, sitting down and slid over on the red leatherette banquette.

"I'm sick of them," Eugene says to C.W. "I'm sick of you!" he screams directly across the table at the women.

"Don't get violent on us now," Donna says, leaning over toward him, while Renee says, "Call him 'Herb.' It really gets him if you call him 'Herb.' "

"I'll kill you," Eugene says.

"Oh, for pity's sakes," C.W. says in a disgusted voice as a waitress finally gets around to their table. "Hi, I'm Lily," the waitress says as she deals out a handful of giant plastic menus and ships water glasses skidding one after the other across the damp sponged-off table.

"Hey, look, Dad," Eugene says, talking like C.W. in one of C.W.'s funny voices and thumbing toward the waitress. "Here's another one for you."

C.W. leans his forehead on his hand and prongs his fingers

into his temples. The women snatch up the menus and Renee announces all around the table, "Hooray for us! We're on vacation! Wouldn't you call this vacation, Donna? Can't you say this trip passes for a vacation?"

Donna has turned over the menu to look at the dessert photos.

Eugene slides his water glass around on the Formica table-top.

He fires it from end to end and catches it just before it flies all the way off the table, then he shoves it from palm to palm until the ice melts down into little opals. Soon the women and C.W. slide out of the banquette and troop happily over to the salad bar.

"Where'd you meet them?" Eugene finally says in a low voice to C.W., who is the first one back with a heaping plate of salad. "Where could anybody meet anyone like them? They're horrible."

"You're horrible," Renee says, instantly appearing with Donna and her own idea of a salad—Jell-O, carrot sticks, and a goblet of tapioca pudding.

"Just kind of ran into them." C.W. smiles, rubbing peace-fully with his thumb at the waxy lip-gloss mark Donna has left on his bottle of lite draft. "I don't exactly know, Eugene, to tell the truth. I like them though. Ladies, you tell me—where'd we meet?"

"Can't remember," Donna says.

"Look at these dog earrings, C.W.," Renee says, starting to give C.W. a neck rub with one hand. "I almost forgot I had them on. I thought they kind of looked like A & W, you know, with his spots? You see that, Eugene?"

"Get those things out of my face," Eugene says, beginning to notice everybody's food.

"Eugene, you ever see anything like this before?" C.W. says, chuckling lightly and pointing his spoon from one of the women to the other and bending his neck around for Renee's neck rub. "Personally, I never saw anything like these two."

"We are a crazy pair," Renee says, grinning. "Always been best friends too, haven't we, Donna?"

"Saw the stupidest dog out there when we were coming in," Eugene says, eating tapioca off of Renee's plate, almost beginning to tranquilize himself, to simmer down a little, with the spoon action slipping in and out of his mouth.

"What color?" C.W. says, lazily throwing his arms back over the rear of the banquette and resting his legs crossed at the ankles up on the seat across from him.

"Some lady's poodle," Eugene says.

"Clipped or what? Woolly or gussied up? Bows? No bows? What color? Be specific," C.W. says.

"Who cares?" Eugene says. "It was a poodle."

"Poodles are smart dogs, Eugene," Renee says. "Don't you be putting poodles down now."

"You'd never want a poodle. Would you ever want a poodle, Dad?" Eugene says.

"Don't know," C.W. says. "I'd have to see it before I'd know. How could I say if I hadn't even had a chance to see the darn thing."

"Poodles are dogs too, Eugene, you know," Donna says.

"I can't believe you, Dad. I can't believe you."

Eugene swipes up his pop can and heads outside through the revolving door. He stomps a few hundred yards up and down the roadside. Then skidding his heels down into the mud-banked ditches, Eugene elbows his way through swarming dragonflies and bunches of pussy willow and goldenrod, through weeping willow branches, until C.W. appears against a white-bread sky as plain as the no-pattern pattern of Stardust's fur and he yells down at him in the ditch, "Son! We ordered you some chocolate layer mud-pie shit whether you want it or not. We got to all try and stay happy on this trip. So come on back inside now. The ladies are saying that they are beginning to miss you. Hell, Eugene."

The story on the gig is that it's just a shorty, a fill-in stint for the weekend at the Resort Red Apple, a sometime family but mostly convention site housed in a huge rambling frame building with a couple of loads of road gravel raked across the front. There is a convention of sports-coated tire salesmen with their wives along—the men listening to each other talk all morning and then dressing themselves up in crazy pants to play golf in the afternoon sun, while their wives, dressed in simple silky dresses and high-heeled pumps, go first to a luncheon fashion show and then spend the rest of the afternoon slipping their legs one way and then slipping their legs the other way while sitting on folding chairs hearing about flower arranging in a corner of the lobby.

Also at the Red Apple are a couple of big family reunions, some honeymooners, and even it's the once-a-year weekend for a gathering of enthusiasts for a Psychic Faire that sets up on card tables in the low-rent space down in the basement with its chipped checkerboard-tiled flooring, an adjacent hot-breathing laundry room, and a nice variety of vending machines.

At night in the enormous dining room, C.W.'s band plays big-band dance music underneath a slowly turning mirrored mosaic ball that showers the dancers and band over with a fine sprinkling of tiny lights, and during the afternoon, C.W. slugs it out with the boys in rehearsal.

The women get bored.

They lie coiled in deck chairs out by the pool looking for

something to happen. They rub cocoa-butter squares over their lips and shake up bottles of baby oil and iodine just to see how long it takes them to separate again into a layer of oil and a layer of iodine. They look in on Eugene from time to time, knocking on his door, and once inside they talk about C.W., about how they need him to take them on some horses or up in the gondola. They follow the signs to the Psychic Faire and they spend time down there, down in the basement, slapping down the cool tile steps in their rubber pool sandals to wander around in the smoggy incense haze, their fists jammed deep in their pockets holding quarters for the vending machines.

Eugene hangs out mostly in his room of the seen-better-days suite C.W. paid money and upgraded them all to. He sits by the window in the armless rocker, holding his trumpet, dressed in khakis and clunky oxfords, his socks left smelly and accordioned on the bathroom floor. Jumbled up on the windowsill, faintly contaminating things, are some of the little gewgaws left over from the various invasions of the women; there is a ring with a colored stone bought somewhere on one of their stops in the French Peugeot, a corncob pipe bought who knows where, a pair of "him and her" wooden outhouse salt and pepper shakers, and a key ring with a crystal held on by wire-reinforced dried bird claws.

There are also boxes of Famous Fudge Factory fudge stacked all around his room—such as on the TV, on the bedside table, stuffed back over in the corner—from the original Famous Fudge Factory that sends out catalogues and mailers and fudge all over the country, made with the secret ingredient Renee immediately recognized as your basic store-bought Eagle Brand condensed milk. "It even has the recipe on the side of the can. I can make that stuff myself," she said in a loud voice as they all had stood and watched while a hairnetted fudge lady, with tendrils of frizz seeping out of a webby hairnet, slid out a fresh batch smooth onto real Italian marble in one masterful pour. It was utterly gorgeous to Eugene and shining with bumpy nuts—he could not take his eyes off the stuff—while C.W., oblivious to such tourist-trappish beauty, was squatted down on the floor and was rubbing the ears of a blind yellow Lab, an old girl dog, and saying, "Look at this here, Eugene. Can't you just feel your blood pressure going down? Mine is."

Eugene does his horn work until his chops grind to a lactic-acid-imposed halt. When that happens, he knocks off and moves the rabbit ears around on the TV set and kicks back with a box of the fudge to wait for chop recovery with the talk shows. He draws faces and stars on the soles of his shoes with the hotel ballpoint pen and thinks about when the next time is finally going to be to start another mighty, no-screwing-around, serious, going-for-it practice session, where you start and do the whole thing straight through, no breaks.

To Eugene, being here at the Resort Red Apple is actually pretty close to being in his own room back at home—what with the horn practice, the shoe-sole art, the TV—although minus the fudge and minus, of course, his dad and minus the women.

Killing time, his chops still out of commission, Eugene rocks back in the armless rocker, reaches his legs out, and studies the wild geometric carpeting, its oranges bumped up a notch or two by vibrant sloshes of molten light sloshed out from the fiery sun just now out the window cannonballing its mega-self wholeheartedly down in a mercury sky. Mindlessly, snaking his arm over to the box of fudge to pinch off another glob, Eugene looks over his music, reading again the neat pencil markings made there by his teacher and again checking on its order so he is sure to start with the lip slurs, then move on to the intervals, and then get in the melodic études—all this the foundation, the very same foundation, that made Don Palladino into DON PALLADINO, the sturdy building blocks Eugene must have in place before he can get *any*where with his most recent challenge he pleaded and begged for at his last lesson, the difficult yet exhilarating "The Carnival of Venice."

Cradling his horn, the roof of his mouth stuccoed with fudge, Eugene thinks about C.W.—C.W. off in rehearsal. Then Eugene thinks this: that he never thought his dad would turn out to be like this; that he never really thought much about his dad turning out at all. He thought his dad *had* turned out.

After a while, there's nothing more to think about that, he's thought it all, so Eugene switches thought gears and checks again to see how the lactic acid is dispersing within him. He runs his tongue over to take a reading on the state of his lips. He reaches for some Vaseline. He squeezes off another piece of fudge, then drops the fudge back into the fudge box and rummages under a pile of old newspapers on the floor to feel for the little sheet of waxed paper that goes on top before the lid. Things are not bad, actually, Eugene thinks, what with the women off someplace else, not here, and with only the maid occasionally wanting to get at his bed or mop around in his bathroom.

Donna and Renee are at that instant at the door, kicking it with their feet.

Eugene starts from staring out the window. He sighs heavily. Next he experiences a short drifting nostalgic spell of wondering about Iris.

"Eugene, open up. Eugene? Get the door!" Donna or Renee shouts from outside in the hall.

"Just a minute," Eugene answers as he ambles into the bathroom, his unlaced oxfords slipping down off his bare heels.

The women do more kicking on his door and thud it with their shoulders. "Open up. This stuff's heavy," one of them yells.

Eugene, in the bathroom, runs rust-colored water full blast in the sink until the rust color pales close enough to regular color, which takes a while. Then he leans his head over to rinse his mouth out, cupping his hand—this a positive, getting-ready kind of step to do, no matter what, with or without the women—before he can continue on with his horn work.

The women keep up their kicking and yelling outside his door.

Eugene swallows some tap water and checks up close in the mirror to see the roof of his mouth. He pulls on his lower lip and groans loudly. He goes back next to the window and drops back down in the armless rocker, then picks up his horn to doodle out a few bars of Arban. He lays his wrist across his thigh and lets his trumpet angle down between his legs.

The women keep it up at the door. Eugene sighs again, tapping his finger on the bell of his horn. He gets up and ambles over to the door to look at the rattling doorknob. Next, he lifts his horn, takes a huge breath, and smacks a high C sharp like he did back at the gas station, holding it until his face goes red, then white, then red again. Outside the women go wild.

Donna glowers in, carrying a stack of carry-out tinfoil containers and a six-pack of orange Nehi. Renee follows with several deep-fat-fried-smelling bags and a wad of napkins. They each have beach bags and are wearing swingy bathing-suit covers zipped over their bathing suits.

"Quit blatting your trumpet, Eugene," Renee says. "Everybody's sick of you out there."

"Fine. Leave. Tell them I'll play quieter," Eugene says, sniffing in their direction because they smell like baby oil mixed with Psychic Faire patchouli.

"Eugene, you're going to get us thrown out of here," Renee

says, as they each put their food containers on Eugene's un-made bed.

"You think I care?" Eugene says.

Donna has rummaged her cowboy boots out of a beach bag and is sitting down on the bed fighting and stomping them on.

"Leave," Eugene says to her. "Leave, leave, leave."

Soon she is marching around the room touching and putting her hands on things. Seeing the TV in the corner, its volume turned low so it's only spiking up bass notes, she sings out, "Hooray for Hollywood!" and trampolines across Eugene's bed to turn up the sound.

"Leave," Eugene says.

"Why?" Donna says, getting ahold of the TV clicker.

Eugene lifts up his horn and he plays a hefty scale, descending chromatically to the lowest possible F sharp. When he finishes, he climbs into the bed with his shoes on, holding his horn, and slides down under the sheets and sits there cross-legged. "Keep your stupid boots off my bed and turn off the TV and get the hell out of here," he says to the women, "or I'll blow your eardrums into the middle of your spongy brains. I can do it, too."

"Herb," Donna says, "you know, you're going to get us all thrown out of here. Probably they're coming now."

The phone rings.

"Ice," Eugene says, picking up the phone, and pointing his finger at Renee, and then at the door.

"See? That's them now," Renee says.

The phone is Iris.

"Stardust is dead," Iris says. "I tried, honey, I got him to the vet and everything like that. Put your daddy on."

"He's not here, Grandma," Eugene says.

"Oh no," Iris says.

"He's left me with these dumb women," Eugene says.

"Oh no," Iris says. "Well, that 57 dog and A & W—is he the bushy one, Eugene? Well, they are fighting it out in the front yard. Listen. I'll put the phone up next to the window screen. Can you hear all that racket? It's a big terrible dog fight."

"Call Mom, Grandma. Call the police," Eugene says.

"Is that Iris?" Donna says. "I want to talk to Iris. I just love Iris!"

"Buzz off," Eugene says to her.

"Hi, Iris! Tell her Hi from me," Renee says.

"And one of the inside dogs," Iris says, continuing on, "little Chili Dog—I now got yellow scallops on my dining-room wall right under the front windows."

"Give me the phone, 'Erb," Donna says, grabbing the phone away from Eugene. "I want to talk to Iris."

"Hi, Iris!" Donna says.

"Pretty good," Donna says.

"Not much," she says.

"C.W.'s rehearsing, he's always rehearsing. We're the only singles here. There's a lot of men with wives, that sort of thing. We run into them everywhere. Then we got old Eugene, of course, but he's—well, he's Eugene, so you can imagine."

"Tell her about the Psychic Faire," Renee says.

"Iris," Donna says, "there's a Psychic Faire here. Do you want us to ask them anything for you? They got that famous psychic that solves police cases."

"That's just what we think too," Donna says.

"Renee and I, we've been thinking we're going to go down there and set us up one of those card tables like they all got— we could rake in some moolah ourselves."

"Pine-Sol," Donna says.

"You did right," Donna says.

"I would have done the same," Donna says. "You know, if he's going to have all those dogs—"

"Okay, okay, okay, okay. Okay, bye," she says, handing the phone back over to Eugene, who's back on the bed making giant bedspring noises rolling over one way to get to the phone and then making giant bedspring noises rolling over the other way to hang up the phone and then making giant bedspring noises rolling all around to get his elbows braced under him so he can get himself up into sitting position with the pillows stuffed solidly up behind his back. When Eugene's all settled, he lifts up his trumpet and attempts to finger the big finale of "The Carnival of Venice," all the while keeping an eye on the women, who are busy going through the carry-out bags and then placing containers of food in a semicircle all around him, murmuring insults.

Until he can get rid of the women and on with his work, Eugene places his horn in its velvet-lined case, affixes all the latches, and gently lowers it to the floor, sliding it all the way safely under the bed. He next thumps his hand around in the sheets looking for a fork to jump up. Then he bites a hole in a salad-dressing packet and squeezes out long, looping strings of salad dressing on top of his salad.

"Here, Eugene, try out my new salt shaker on your chicken," Renee says, dropping her outhouse salt shaker on the bed next to him as she passes by to go over and twist the channel knob on the TV. "I want to see if any salt really comes out of that thing."

Eugene peels butter pats while the women settle down cross-legged on the carpeting, centering their backs up against the foot of his bed. They crack open a fresh box of Famous Fudge Factory fudge and get absorbed in a love matchmaking show and then ride on with their attention spans through to the beginning of a talk show featuring a team of male strippers just back from a smash tour across Europe.

. . .

The first thing C.W. sees as he unlocks the door and sings out "Dudes!" is Donna absently licking her palms and fingers and rolling around on the floor in front of the TV, knees to chest.

Inside the room, in the flickering light from the TV, the close air has developed a gelatinous, fish-tank quality, complete with unhealthy granules moving slowly throughout it.

"Dogs are all over the house," Donna is saying, not noticing C.W. "Iris's going to let the dogs go out on the road. Are you listening to this, Eugene?"

"You mean 'Erb, don't you?" Renee says, sucking fudge off of each of her fingers.

Eugene, gnawing on his third ear of corn, is lying back on the bottom sheet of the bed, with his top sheet and spread wadded and stuffed together down at the foot. "What do I care?" he is saying. "I don't care."

"Dudes!" C.W. sings out again, having to yell loud over the TV to be even noticed.

"Dad! You're back!" Eugene says, his head snapping up off the pillows.

"Of course I'm *back*. What'd you think? I wasn't coming back, that I wouldn't be coming back?" C.W. says, catching sight of the TV and fanning the room door back and forth to stir around the air.

"C.W.! Where've you been?" Donna says, patting the floor for C.W. to come and sit next to her, all the while keeping one eye on the male strippers tying bandannas around their necks, readying themselves for something big. "Come over here, C.W. You won't believe what we found on the TV."

"Oh no," C.W. says, twisting his mouth around and talking out of the side in his funny voice. "Change the channel, ladies. Jesus Christ, what are we watching here? My God, but it's a bunch of faggolas parading around on daytime TV despoiling the housewives. Here, I'll help you out with that, Donna. Hand me over the clicker. Where's the clicker? My God, but are you sitting your butt on top of the clicker?"

"See, Dad," Eugene says. "Get them out of here."

"You're not touching this clicker, C.W.," Donna says, gluing herself onto the clicker.

"Me and Donna are thinking we are going to get you and that lump of bad humor over there to put us on a show, C.W.," Renee says, winking over at Eugene.

"Go right ahead, Dad," Eugene says, tossing a corncob into the bathroom underhanded.

"I hate those commercials where they use real people," Donna says as a real person has appeared on the screen to do a commercial.

"That guy should be licensed or regulated or something," Renee says.

"Okay. Okay. Okay, kids, enough. What's this about Iris and my dogs?" C.W. says. "Let's get serious here."

"Stardust got hit by a hot-rodder, and Iris is fed up with everything, so she's going to let them go loose out on the road," Renee says.

C.W. slouches into the doorframe and crosses his hiking boots at the ankles. The women return themselves wholeheartedly to the TV screen as the strippers come back on and start flouncing around the stage flexing their muscles rhythmically to what sounds like somebody backstage hitting with a metal hammer on the studio safe.

There is some interesting, innovative camera work.

"Well, C.W., keep working out on that Nautilus machine," Donna sighs.

"What a snotty attitude," Eugene says, rummaging around in one of his carry-out bags for something else to eat.

"All right, ladies, here's the skinny, ladies," C.W. says, stepping resolutely into the middle of the room. "I'll spell it out for you straight up. I am almost a half century old and I'm not interested in performing any striptease right this minute. Later, maybe, if you can stand it I can stand it, so who knows? But for now, I'm bushed. I'm beat. I need an hour or so to zone out, to rest myself in this deluxe suite I have arranged for all of us before I have to go and deal with calling Iris and finding what's going on with my dogs, and then there's those tire salesmen probably going to ask for 'Moon River' all night." He looks at the clock.

"Go, Dad!" Eugene says. "Go to your room. Rest up, watch TV, zone out. Just take your women with you."

"No," Donna says. "This is the only room with a TV that works."

"Oh, Jesus," C.W. says. "I guess I don't really even have all that much time to rest. I really have to handle things with Iris."

"I need to work on my music," Eugene says.

"I want to go up in the gondola," Renee says.

"That'd be fun," Donna says.

"I hear you," C.W. says. "I hear you. We'll try to fit the gondola in before we shove off in the morning. If we're up and packed and out of here early—"

"C.W.? But we wanted to take you down for a session with the psychics," Renee says.

"I don't want to know any more," C.W. says.

"Come on, C.W.! They don't ever tell you anything bad," Donna says.

"I guess," C.W. says. "Okay. When can we fit in the psychics? Let's see." The women go back to the TV. "If I cut my nap back," C.W. continues, "and if we're all dressed—look, ladies? Here's the story. Listen. I can't deal with all this time management and the gondola and the mess in this room and what everybody wants to do and the dogs and the band and the tire salesmen and now fag strippers and also fruitcake psychics. I am only one person. I am only one human being."

"So am I," Donna says. "And this is my vacation."

"So am I," Eugene says. "And I will never play 'Moon River' for anybody, ever."

"Oh, for Pete's sake," C.W. says.

"Get them out so I can practice," Eugene says.

"I hear you. I hear you," C.W. says. "Eugene? You sure you don't want to take them up in the gondola? You have any interest in doing that, son?"

"None. Zip. Uh-uh."

"Okay. Okay. Hold on. Let me think. Just a minute, *please*, ladies. We'll work something out. Ladies? Would you want to go alone? I'll fund it, the whole thing."

"No. We want you. We want *you*, C.W."

"Okay. Okay," C.W. says. "Let's start somewhere. Let's start with our schedule. I want you all to know our schedule. We have to handle the schedule thing."

Donna and Renee and Eugene look up at C.W., all of them scrambled over with soft hotel-room shadows.

"We got a little space of time," C.W. says, pointing to the clock, "before we have to be completely, totally, absolutely, completely dressed and ready to step out that door you see over there. That means *all* our makeup on. That means *all* our eyes all done and everything else whatever that may be for each of us—and our hairdos all fixed like we like them and sprayed and us downstairs and ready for me to go to work. If you are ready on time, we can drop by the psychics . . . but briefly, briefly, do you hear? Then you will be all set so you can see the show starring—?"

"It'd never be you," Eugene mumbles.

"C.W.!" the women shout in unison.

"And," says Renee, "we got ourselves a couple of drop-dead dresses to wear for your event tonight!"

"We brought us killer dresses!" Donna screams.

"Right on, ladies!" C.W. says, raising his fist into the air. "Right on!"

Using Eugene's head for support, Donna trampolines across the bed, stepping over corncobs, chicken bones, peas, biscuit parts, and a logjam of French fries. "Just don't touch the channel knob on the TV, keep away from the clicker while I'm gone, 'Erb," she says as she giant-steps over Eugene, not meaning to but flinging his head from side to side as she executes a neat little bent-kneed jump off the bed.

"I'll guard the clicker, Donna," Renee says.

"Don't fall in," C.W. says, sitting down on the bed beside Eugene like he used to when Eugene was a little kid and they were going to have what passed for them as a father-son heart-to-heart.

"Son," C.W. says quietly, "I hate to say it, but it looks like it's here we got to be, so move over your lunch containers and give your poor old tired dad some room."

"Why?" Eugene says. "Just give me one good reason why."

C.W. picks up one of his feet and starts unlacing his boot and peeling off his sock. He sighs deeply, looking off out the window at the big gondola moving slowly up the mountain. Then he stretches his body out on the bed alongside Eugene and starts working his hips solidly into the mattress and messing his toes into Renee's hair down at the foot of the bed, where Renee is consumed with TV watching.

"Son, listen to me," C.W. says to Eugene in a low voice. "I don't want to be in charge here. I hate this being-in-charge stuff."

Donna slams open the bathroom door, klieg-lighting the room with high-watt bathroom light. C.W. and Eugene turn to look at her for a second.

"I just got to have a break so I can get on with the next event," C.W. goes on, fumbling in his breast pocket and shoving on his aviators.

Donna heads straight across the room and makes them undulate up and down as she steps up on the bed and wallows over the both of them, laughing and saying down at C.W. "Oh, you—" because he's grabbed on to her ankles with both his hands.

"This is my room," Eugene says evenly. "I am not vacating this room. You are not taking over my room along with everything else on the planet, like my practice time, all of my life, all of life," he says.

"Oh, Eugene. You faker," Donna says, throwing him a little grin back over her shoulder as she jumps off the bed and settles in with Renee down in front of the TV.

C.W. smiles over at Eugene and tugs on one of his pants belt loops. "Okay, dude," he says, "We hear you. Nobody's going to take your whole life. Come on, now. Ease up."

Somehow Eugene actually gets caught up in the TV show. The male strippers actually get sort of interesting even to Eugene. It's during the interview part of the show when the strippers are telling about how they each got to where they are in life—like how some certain event happened, and then something else unexpected came along, and then what they did after that—until the next unexpected thing happened. Eugene sees a kind of pattern emerging—personal action, then unexpected event, then personal action, then unexpected thing—all of which for the male strippers lead up to them being strippers being interviewed on this TV show today. Eugene relaxes a little and starts thinking. He turns himself around down to the foot of the bed and rolls over on his stomach to rest his head on a bunched-up feather pillow to better see the TV.

"I thought there would be time for things on this vacation, son, you know," C.W. cranks up monotonously alongside

Eugene, just as Eugene is beginning to maybe unravel something applicable to life.

"I thought we would get away," C.W. drones on, "raise hell,
go wild, laugh a lot. I saw us doing that—slapping our arms
around each other, running wild, women hanging off of us.
You get that picture, Eugene? Can you see us like that? Envision it as I envisioned it." C.W. lies quiet beside Eugene for
a while, breathing deeply, envisioning.

"Are you with me?" C.W. says.

"Almost. Just be quiet," Eugene says.

"God, I still can," C.W. says. "I still can envision it. It's clear
as day. What do you think that means?"

Eugene is trying to stay with his own thoughts, is trying to
hold C.W. separate in one part of his mind and listen and hang
with what the male strippers are saying in the other part of his
mind.

"How I saw it, when I got this idea for all of us," C.W. says,
"is I thought this would be a good mix of just good people. No
big deal. Us two cool dudes showing two up-for-anything
ladies some fun. I wasn't just going toward nothing, Eugene.
I wasn't just popping us all off without a plan."

"Okay, okay," Eugene says, nodding his head.

"I didn't *know* I was going to be working all the time. I
didn't *know* the TV would be broken in my room. Mostly, I
didn't know there would be no time. That's the biggie as I see
it. There is just no time."

"I know. I know. I know," Eugene says.

"Man, Eugene, we can't seem to get anything done, can we?
I haven't even called Iris. I haven't even gone to sleep yet."

"Okay, okay, okay," Eugene says, nodding and looking
sympathetic back at his dad.

"Iris always says to me, 'Keep it to one dog.' But I'm only
giving things a try, you know. If you don't try—Did you hear

what I just said, Eugene?" C.W. says, lifting up his head to make sure the women aren't listening. The women are in their own world. They are still completely one with the male strippers.

Then C.W., dropping his head back down and sighing heavily, says to Eugene, "Now you tell me, Eugene, how is it that we could even have to contend with even TV fag strippers after we got them this suite? What do those TV scum wads have?"

"Okay, okay, okay," Eugene says.

C.W. works himself up and yells down at the women, "How long's that show going to go anyway, ladies? Is that the new fag twenty-four-hour station you got there or what?"

A room service cart rattles down the hall. There is a knocking on the door next door.

"Okay, the strippers are gone," Donna says, as on the TV screen appears a closing close-up shot of each of the strippers with the credits being run over their faces. "Let's think of something to do. You feeling better now, C.W.?"

"Oh, Renee," C.W. says, moaning the words, "oh, sweet Jesus in heaven, we *are* doing something."

"But you've been gone all day," Renee says. "We sit around like this at home, waiting to put the babies to bed and then waiting to get the babies up out of bed. This is no big whoop-de-do for me and Donna, you know. Our whole life is waiting."

"I know it. I know it," C.W. says in an irritated voice that makes Eugene remember his old living-at-home dad before his dad became this new, single, fun dad.

"Like what would you two want to do?" Eugene says. "Neither of you can *do* anything."

"Screw off, Eugene," Renee says.

"Screw off, Herb," Donna says.

"You screw off!" Eugene says back at them.

"Shut up, Eugene," Donna says.

"You! Shut! Up!" Eugene says, pulling his chest up on the pillow and shouting salady onion breath into a spot on Renee's scalp. Renee jumps up and runs over to the door and starts fanning it back and forth to get Eugene's bad-breath smell out of the room.

"No, buddy! You! Shut! Up!" Donna says, as C.W. is ripping off his shades and screaming out, "For pity's sake!"— which starts their neighbor banging on the wall over next to the bed, which makes C.W., Eugene, Donna, and Renee freeze and listen, and then soon, slowly, all simmer down, settle back down, and all sink back into the noise level the neighbor and the rest of the hotel guests all seemed to tolerate okay enough before.

C.W. works the toes of one foot deep into Donna's hair and the toes of the other foot deep into Renee's hair and then tries to hold them still down at the foot of the bed with strong toe grips. He says to Eugene, "I was thinking down there, buddy, that you'd probably snaked these women away from me by now." Then he positions his shades up on his forehead and trails his fingers up and down under his shirt.

"Okay, here's what we'll do," Renee says, suddenly reaching around behind her head and holding on to C.W.'s foot like she is struck by some giant thought. "Donna will go first and then I will go and then you, Eugene, you can tell us which is the best. Then you'll get a turn and we'll be the audience for you. C.W., you just forget about us and go on and get you some sleep. You need it, buddy."

"Just try to do whatever you're going to do quietly, okay? Show some mercy, ladies," C.W. says. "Renee, try rubbing my foot a little bit, okay, Renee? Since you've got ahold of it, okay?"

"Best at what?" Eugene says, leaning off the bed from the waist up to check underneath where his horn is stored in its hard case, all its latches latched, getting its beauty sleep. "Neither of you can *do* anything."

"They can give feet jobs," C.W. murmurs, fixing his shades back over his eyes, already drifting. "Don't be afraid of your knuckles, Renee."

"We're going to do towel fashions!" Donna announces, doing a little tumbler spring up onto her feet.

Eugene drops his head down so he is puffing and skiddering dust balls around under the bed with his breath. "Oh yeah, well," he says, "I'll be sure to get right on it. Throw me some towels down here, you know, what a great idea. Maid! Maid! Bring us some more towels!" he yells.

"Shut up, Eugene," C.W. says. And then in a reasonable tone, he says, "You know, Eugene, that sounds pretty easy. You just got to lie here and watch the ladies do interesting stuff with towels. Big deal. How hard can that be?"

"Some fun you are, Eugene," Renee says as she turns around and gets up onto her knees and knuckles directly into C.W.'s arch.

"Do you *ever* have any fun, Eugene?" Donna says.

"Ladies, please, don't start up with him. Just do your show if it'll make you happy," C.W. says, pulling his foot out of Renee's grip.

The women stand up and brush off their rears before stepping up on the bed to trampoline across. Eugene fears for his spine and thinks of C.W. lying next to him with those sunglasses, with his very eyesight at risk of them putting a foot through one of the lenses or one of them coming crashing down on top of him, messing him up in several ways at once, hell, messing them both up, father and son, spines, eyes, stomach stomped in, windpipes crushed, balls squashed flat. While

Eugene is thinking of these things, the women jump off the bed with neat little gym-class tumbler jumps, traipse across the room with springy knee action, slam the bathroom door, and make their usual loud locking noises.

"Turn off the TV," Eugene yells, still facing under the bed. "Donna, get the TV. Donna! The tube!" Another room service or maid cart rumbles down the hall outside their door. A heavy custodial door slams somewhere with a *wham!*

"Eugene," C.W. mumbles. "Son, wake me up, you know, if they do anything—good."

The women start running water and making drawer opening and closing noises. Eugene, hanging half off the bed, heaves himself upright and kicks a gnawed corncob so it spins across the room and hits the bathroom door.

"Don't come in," says one of the women from inside.

"Turn off the TV," Eugene yells. "Get the TV, Renee. We want it quiet in here."

"It's okay, son. Listen to me," C.W. says while folding his shades neatly and sliding them into their case. "If this is the biggest problem you got in your life, by which I mean sleeping with the TV on because you can't get a couple of women to leave off what they're doing—which is getting ready to run around in towels just for your personal pleasure and enjoyment—then you've got a hell of a life, kiddo." C.W. slips his hand down in his pants, then he pulls his hand out of his pants, then he flips over onto his stomach and windmills his arms and legs out into a sleep-awaiting sprawl. Eugene sits himself up higher and straighter on the bed so that he's sitting straight up against the headboard, his knees compacted to his chest. He watches C.W. uneasily, trying not to notice C.W.'s face loosening and softening as C.W. starts letting go into sleep.

C.W. starts snoring.

Eugene picks at the cuticle on his thumb, then bites off a

long fingernail. He looks everywhere around the room. Nothing good is on the TV.

After a while, Eugene decides to try and work a dangerous-looking chicken bone out from under where he's noticed C.W.'s half lying on it. C.W. suddenly scares Eugene by windmilling around the other way and rolling all by himself off of the chicken bone. Eugene quickly swipes up the chicken bone and sticks it in the breast pocket of his own shirt.

Next, C.W. starts breathing weirdly so his chest goes up and down real fast, like he's fighting for breath but with no air getting in his lungs. Then, suddenly, C.W. gasps and gulps and starts making enormous loud snorting sounds as he finally succeeds in filling his lungs with air, again and again sucking in air, gulping up lungfuls of precious air, then gasping a few more times and pretty soon sinking back into a normal sleep.

C.W. goes through this same routine several more times. After a handful of these interludes, in which C.W. seems to Eugene to get it together just as death by suffocation is upon him, Eugene decides that there is a pattern to all this and begins timing C.W.'s episodes with his watch for something to do. He slumps down on the bed, wedges his trumpet case under his knees, and writes down the time of each interlude on the heel of his shoe with the hotel ballpoint pen.

In between a couple of interludes, Eugene pulls open the bedside-table drawer to get to one of the last of the Famous Fudge Factory fudge boxes—this one labeled "penuche." He can hear the women bucking around in the bathroom.

Eugene starts slashing at the cellophane with the hotel ballpoint pen. He makes a decision not to look at C.W. anymore or time his episodes or anything. Except from time to time he is forced to look if only to see if C.W.'s maybe looking at him.

. . .

Donna cracks open the bathroom door. Light lasers in, bisecting Eugene. He has the fudge box sitting on top of his stomach and is darting his tongue around inside his mouth trying to mold a glob of penuche fudge flat across his front teeth. Donna whispers to him, "Put on some music, Eugene. Here's Renee's blaster."

Eugene keeps working on the fudge, ignoring her, trying to get it to mold into a small fang in the middle. Finally, Donna just stalks out barefooted with Renee's blaster, wearing a couple of washcloths safety-pinned to the elastic of her underpants along with a scarf twisted up tight around her chest, water-ballooning the top half of her breasts out the top. She goes over to the table and clatters some cassettes around, knocking a bunch off onto the floor. Eugene watches to make sure she isn't doing anything to any of his music or to anything else of his.

Renee follows, dressed like Donna. She comes prancing across the room and pivots swiftly, circling around the foot of the bed to slouch in front of Eugene, one scabby knee from their filling-station fight slightly bent.

"How long is this going to take?" he whispers.

"Come on, Eugene," Donna whispers back, glaring at him.

He grins at her so the fudge shows molded across his front teeth just as C.W. starts breathing weirdly again, so his chest goes rapidly up and down, followed by gasps and gulps for air, then the final loud choking, snorting noises that Eugene knows by now mean "all clear." Then back to normal sleep.

"What's that?" Donna says, pointing her index finger down at C.W.

"That's how he sleeps," Eugene whispers.

Donna prances smartly across the room, scissoring her skinny legs, and stares down at both C.W. and Eugene, looking back and forth from one to the other.

"What took you so long?" Eugene says to Renee, grinning

wider so his teeth show even better with the fudge fang. "Donna beat you getting out here."

"I shaved my legs. Wake him up," she says, pointing to C.W., who's moving around like he is threatening to start up again.

"He's scary like that," Donna says.

"He's worse awake," Eugene says, as they all stare down at C.W. "We got to let him sleep."

"Shut up, shut up, shut up," C.W. says out loud. "Shut up all of you," he says, and rolls over so his leg is smack up alongside Eugene's leg.

The women squat down on the floor.

Eugene whispers, "Okay? You women done? Those men strippers on TV leave you guys in the dust."

"Shut up, Eugene," Donna whispers, undoing her scarf where it's slipped down a little, and then redoing it up tighter so her breasts wrinkle together and balloon like before out the top. "Come on, Renee, let's go try another outfit."

"Try one over your face," Eugene whispers.

"Shut up, I'm telling you, all of you, shut up," C.W. says out loud again.

They freeze.

"You go, Eugene," Renee mouths, squatting down even lower on the floor beside the side of the bed and mouthing her lips next to Eugene's ear. "You go. Come on, Eugene."

"Quit breathing on me," Eugene says. "You're breathing on me."

"Do it, Eugene, whatever it is," C.W. says in a normal voice. "For God's sakes, whatever it is, just do it."

Eugene flails around in the covers, jostling C.W., and leans off the side of the bed to stuff his trumpet case back underneath. "Just give me some towels. I'll *do* it," he says, standing up out of the bed and fumbling with his belt buckle to show them how serious he is about doing this thing. With his khakis unzipped and hanging on just by his hipbones, Eugene duck-walks into the bathroom. "I'm going to do it," he mouths back over his shoulder. "I'm going," he says, shutting the bathroom door and making loud locking noises.

"Just stay the fuck out of here," C.W. says.

The women grin. They clap their hands soundlessly. Donna clutches her breasts and rolls, vertebra by vertebra, backwards onto the bed beside C.W., her hair spreading out rippled like a high-fashion shampoo ad. Renee sits herself carefully on the bed beside Donna and C.W., being careful not to bump any part of C.W. She slides the penuche fudge box over in front of her and Donna.

"Look at the skin on his nose," Donna whispers to Renee when C.W. is snoring nicely again.

"What is it with this fudge and soda pop and us? Look, I got fat rolls already," Donna whispers.

"We should be calling home to check on the babies," Renee mouths. They both look over at the phone.

After a while, Donna gets up and pads across the room to kick the bathroom door a couple of times. "Let's have it, Eugene," she whispers, her mouth up against the door. "Make it good."

She climbs back up on the bed.

Pretty soon, the door opens wide and Eugene stands illuminated bare-chested with a shower cap pulled down low on his head and a towel wrapped around his waist. He has a second towel pinned at the neck so that it flaps out in back capelike as he stomps into the room in his leather oxfords. "Are you happy, you dipshits?" he says to the women. "Is this dumb enough for you, or should I go back in there and get dumber so you'll like it even better?"

C.W. coughs and snorts. He does a sleeping windmill turn.

The women are laughing and stuff wads of the top sheet in their mouths. They try to keep from getting hit by C.W.'s windmilling arms and legs. They lean face down on the bed, laughing, their knobbed spines poking up out of their skinny backs.

"Fuck you," Eugene says, walking over and shoving Renee aside so he can get down on the floor on all fours and fish out his trumpet case from under the bed.

Renee, gathering herself up on her haunches beside C.W., ungags herself and whispers, "Make just one more outfit, *please*, Eugene. Like that one—so we can—at least—pick which—one—is best."

"Okay, here, how's this?" Eugene says, pulling off his waist-wrapped towel so he is dressed in just his Jockeys alone. "How's this for another outfit?"

"We gotta go in the closet," Donna says, in convulsions of laughter, nodding toward C.W. and grabbing Renee by the arm to pull her toward the closet. "We gotta go in the closet."

Eugene drops his head down on his trumpet case and lets his eyes close as the women clamber around and over him. Soon he can hear metal hangers tinging, thumps thudding against the closet walls, the women's muffled voices.

The first thing C.W. sees when he opens his eyes is Eugene in stretched-out Jockeys, his hair water-combed back, standing in front of the closet door blowing on his horn. Eugene has the same ugly, spiky hairline that C.W. has, the same one C.W. has always hated in himself and tried to hide in any way he could think of in the old days and with this latest fancy combing job in the present. As C.W. rises up on one elbow, Eugene is saying to the closet door, "Now what did you think of that, given what I have just explained to you? Is that shit or good?"

"Now listen, Renee," Eugene continues, "Renee, listen up! Donna, you listen in there too. You're part of this." Eugene lifts up his horn and plays a little Tijuana Brass bit and then a bit like you would hear from the horn of, say, a Don Palladino.

"Oh, fuck. They hear nothing," Eugene says to himself, but then he plays the same things again anyway.

"Jesus Christ, Eugene, shut the fuck up," C.W. says, rising up to a sitting position. "Can it up your ass, Eugene."

"Look, ladies! Dad's coming around," Eugene says, aiming his horn at C.W. and starting the beginning of reveille.

"Jesus Christ, shut up, Eugene," C.W. screams while fighting his arms clear of the sheets to reach for the bell of Eugene's horn.

"Do it again, Eugene!" Donna shrieks, throwing back the closet door, which hits the wall and slams closed on her again.

"Don't even think about it, Eugene," C.W. says, making a fist and hitting with it a few times in the palm of his hand.

Eugene points his horn the other way and plays a few more bars of reveille, kind of trailing off at the end.

"C.W.," Renee says, coming out of the closet, "you should have seen Eugene dancing around in here."

"What time is it?" C.W. says, looking wildly all around the room to see a clock.

"Come on, C.W., get you some towels like Eugene," Donna says.

"You better believe it, ladies. You better believe it. And I want to see you too," C.W. says. "But we got to go to work now, so come on. I got you three front and center, close to the best table in the house for the dinner show, with sirloin steaks, twice-baked potatoes, and whatever you want to drink. Special-ordered the whole thing. What do you think of that?"

"Yippee!" the women say.

Donna and Renee pad into the bathroom and start turning

on the faucets in the sink and plugging in their crimping iron and digging out their little beaded evening purses and underthings from their suitcases in the suite's other room.

"All right, Eugene," C.W. says, coming back, holding up his tux in one hand and picking lint-looking particles and strands of fine shiny thread that are actually, under examination, the women's long squiggly hairs off the jacket with the other. "All right, man. Didn't I tell you? Didn't I tell you? You've done a complete one-eighty, haven't you, Eugene? You're coming on like gangbusters, man."

As he bumps the French Peugeot through a pothole getting onto the main road from the Resort Red Apple, C.W. says, "You will notice, ladies, that my gig car here has the most terrific shock absorbers. Now, you look back there at that deep pothole we just crossed, and you hardly knew it, did you?"

"What pothole where?" Renee says from the back seat, where she and Donna and Eugene are sitting three across, sipping the bourbon-sweet sodas they took with them from brunch.

"In fact, this will interest you as well," C.W. carries on gamely as he's wedging his drink into the little plastic car drink-holder accessory he's got installed on the dashboard. "It's these French Peugeots that win all the safari races over there in deepest, darkest Africa, ladies—that kind of thing. Rally races, like that." C.W. goes quiet and grips the steering wheel with both hands, then charges the whining French Peugeot up a narrow entrance ramp, breaks out onto the superhighway, cuts straight across several lanes on a diagonal to get to the fast lane, where the car settles into what it was built to do and bullets along in the sunshine, its hand-rubbed paint job bouncing flaming spit wads back up at the sky.

Eugene is crumpled up between the women, the wind from

the open window slicking his hair flat into Sunday-school parts and beating and foaming up the women's into frothy, free-standing peaks.

"This car is tough as a Mack truck," C.W. continues. "It soothes me, this car. I can't *tell* you what it does for me when I find anything like this car."

"The babies," Renee says, riding with her back pressed flat up against Eugene so her bare feet can fit out the window.

"What's that, sweetheart?" C.W. says, speaking back at Renee in the back seat over his shoulder.

"Nothing. Just something I thought of," Renee says.

"No, tell me. What was it?" C.W. says.

"She is saying," Eugene says, speaking through tender lips from his hard-fought-for early-morning practice session, "that her kid does the same thing for her that this car does for you."

"Oh. I get what she means," C.W. says, brightening even more and slapping blindly in the back seat to reach for some part of Eugene. "Because see, ladies, that's the same thing like I got with Eugene here."

"You can forget that," Eugene says.

"Well, I will not," C.W. says. "Of course I will not forget it."

"You don't have me."

"Well, I do," C.W. says. "I got you like they got their babies. You *are* my baby."

"Not a hope in hell—" Eugene says. "What you got is nothing if you think you got me."

C.W. is quiet. He looks off into a field that banks the highway. He adjusts the electronic outside side mirror with the little inside toggle switch.

"If you think about it," Eugene says, "but you probably don't want to really think much about it. I dare you to really think about it sometime."

"What are you trying to do, Eugene?" C.W. says quietly.

"What are *you?* That's what I've been wondering my whole life. What are *you?*"

"Oh, well," Donna says. "So what. We're going to go back by that fudge place. Who needs more fudge?"

"Get out of here," Renee answers, thinking about C.W. and Eugene, her head lolled back on the seat.

"No," C.W. says, tapping his aviators snug up onto his nose and rotating his shoulder to loosen up a muscle. "Nope. No fudge. Fudge is over. Time to get back to Iris. Time to touch base with Iris. Iris needs us."

"It's Iris that you got," Eugene says. "That's the only one you really got. Your own mother."

"She'll be forever, too," Renee says. "It's hormones or genes or something. I can tell already with us and the babies."

Later, zapping back up the hill, right before their turnoff to Iris's and along the side of the road, C.W. spots the dogs. Their paws look too heavy to be lifted up, the way they look lifting them.

"It's A & W! It's Route 57! There's even Chili Dog," C.W. shouts. "And they got themselves a new greyhound-looking thing they picked up by themselves!"

"Look at that!" Donna says.

"Where?" Renee says, hiking herself up straighter in the back seat and trying to see through the big ruffly collar on her sundress that keeps flying up in her face.

"I can't believe it," C.W. says, swerving over the French Peugeot. "It's the whole pack of them—except for Stardust. Now what do you think the odds of this were, us finding those fellas like this out here?"

"Why don't you just get a cat? Iris isn't going to let you back in the house with those dogs," Donna says.

"Oh, Iris, Iris! Iris gets herself all worked up, then she gets herself calmed down. I know about Iris. Come on now. I got to herd all them in the car here. Hey, dogs! Come here, Chili Dog, come here, boy, hey 7-Eleven!" C.W. says, while coasting the French Peugeot up behind the dogs and screaming out the window so they panic and run out into the middle of the highway. C.W. slams on the emergency, starts the flashers, and runs out into the road after his scattering flock.

"Keep your legs together, Donna," Renee says.

When C.W. pulls the French Peugeot into Iris's driveway, with the dogs rampaging around in the car, Iris comes to stand rock-still outside on her porch holding in one hand a dishrag smelling strong with Pine-Sol.

As soon as C.W. opens the car door, some of the dogs use his lap for leverage for springing out of the car. Iris, staring off at her zinnia bed, makes the smallest of movements, moving only to tap out one of her Camels from a soft pack, while C.W. and the dogs swarm and mill around her to slap through the screen door. Soon there's the sounds of whining and barking and the can opener eating through metal, and plastic dog dishes being picked up and set back down on the floor and dog toenails clicking frantically on kitchen linoleum and C.W. talking baby talk to his dogs.

Eugene opens the trunk of the French Peugeot and starts digging out his horn case while the women are taking their time to unfurl themselves from the back seat. They walk over to Iris, who holds her Camel off to the side, and they wrap her up in their arms and feel how small yet steady she seems to them to be, the way Iris is still perfectly the same, is still in the same place even that she was in when they all left her—back before the trip.

"Hello, girls," Iris says.

"I wish I had you for a mother," Renee says.

Eugene heads off to the side yard and starts burbling some light stuff up and down on his horn. He works in a tight jazz riff, then eases back to the easy burbles.

After jacking their blood sugar up with dog food, the dogs blast out of the house and surge powerfully in a muscled pack around all of the trees and bushes in the yard, stopping frequently to go to the bathroom.

Chili Dog peels off from the pack and climbs up the front steps. He starts scratching at himself, really digging in deep in places with his nails and tiny front teeth. The new greyhound dog that C.W.'s already named Dog Track heads over by Eugene to lie down among the zinnias and start licking himself methodically with his long muscular tongue.

C.W. walks out on the porch carrying some lite brews and a kitchen box of wooden matches. He sits down on one of Iris's wicker chairs and picks Chili Dog up in his lap while he strips the pop-top off a beer and takes half the can in a series of swallows.

"Look, Mom," C.W. says to Iris. "This is funny. Chili Dog's been out there in the wild rolling around in burrs."

"There's a tick nation living under the burrs," Iris says.

Eugene quits with the warm-up stuff and finally moves wholehearted into the finale of "The Carnival of Venice"— after several piercing running tries at it.

C.W. starts striking up matches with the fingers of one hand while holding Chili Dog still with the other hand, then dotting the blown-out match end precisely on top of each bulby tick end.

The women are backing around their little car with the baby seat in the back. They yell up at the porch, "Thanks, you guys! We had a great time!"

C.W. waves out a lit match. "You leaving so soon, ladies?

Well, okay, ladies. See you around. Take it easy. Don't go falling in before we meet up again."

"Don't you either," the women chorus back.

Getting up on his feet with Chili Dog, C.W. yells out, "I aim to hang on with everything I can think of, ladies."

Eugene has started "The Carnival of Venice" over from the very beginning and is proceeding mechanically, with no interpretation at all, through the chop-bursting middle section, trying to iron out the most onerous technical impossibilities note by impossible note.

"We'll bring the babies by to show them to the dogs!" Donna yells, gunning up her sputtering engine and finally hitting first gear.

"Well, there's plenty of them," Iris says, indicating dogs all over the place with her arms.

C.W. holds aloft a lite brew in salute to the women. "Here's to you, ladies. And, also, here's to many more which you richly deserve and shall have out of me as long as I have the strength to raise my arm up in the air! You are the best, ladies—that's exactly what you are!"

"Same to you!" one of the women yells as they drive off, bits of rust from their car flying into Eugene's eyes.

Eugene packs up his horn and carries it up to the front porch, where he has to pick his way in his leather oxfords around sleeping dogs. C.W. sits back down and looks down at Eugene's shoes and says, "Son? Now, why doesn't your mother get you some shoes like people really wear?"

Eugene sits down on the wicker rocker alongside Iris. He props his feet up on the porch railing and taps his shoes together.

Iris reaches over and pats him on his arm.

C.W. props his hiking boots up on the railing. He allows Chili Dog to slide out of his arms and onto the floor.

A few cars pass by.

Sometimes the dogs look up, but this is the end of it. This is all they do, they don't get up or go chase the cars or start barking or anything. A couple of them do curl themselves around Iris's shoes and lick a few halfhearted licks on her ankle before dropping off to sleep all over again. C.W. reaches down and slides them away from Iris when they do that.

A radio is playing music off somewhere, several houses distant, which to the three of them up on the porch makes their silence just more uneasy and silent.

C.W. tips back his brew and clears his throat. He glances over at Iris. He looks down at Airport on the floor at his feet.

"Eugene," C.W. says, sloshing Airport back and forth in her loose skin with his foot. "I just needed to see if I could make it be the way I saw it in my mind. You know, like I told you—us with the women, in the gig car and all." C.W. pulls his aviators out of his breast pocket and starts wiping on the lens with his shirttail. He lights a match with one hand and leans forward to light up a cigarette for Iris.

"I just saw this somewhere," C.W. goes on, waving the match out in long slow swoops. "These guys drinking beer in plaid shirts. There were women hanging on them. There were dogs jumping up and down and being happy all around. These two guys."

Eugene looks out over the shadowy yard.

"I wanted something like that for us," C.W. says. "So you think that's a sin, Eugene, or something?"

"TV," Iris says. "That beer commercial on TV."

C.W. is quiet for a while, thinking.

"But the dogs were in something different," Iris goes on. "I'll remember what if you just give me a sec.

"Oh, well. Who cares," C.W. says. "Now, the French Peugeot, now, that was real. That thing I just saw sitting on the import car lot, you know, not on TV or anything. The French Peugeot, that one's mine."

The radio music weaves in and out among the cicadas, among the driftings of a soft breeze high in the trees, among the sleeping dogs' heavy breathing. The night is the kind of night fast deepening to the shade of C.W.'s bandleader tux, and the moon is floating mosaic ball-like without the mosaics over all their heads.

"Well, wherever I got it," C.W. says, "it seemed like a good enough idea. Shit! It still does! I can't believe it, but I *still* get excited—even after being in the car with you all day and all, you know? What does that mean? What can that mean but that I still got to keep trying?"

"At least you're not holding your breath over your horn playing."

"Speak for yourself, twerp," C.W. says.

The dogs occasionally jerk awake or go over to scratch at the screen door to get in the house and then scratch at the screen door to get back out of the house, all this just to see if their food bowl and their water dish is where it is supposed to be— namely, over by the oven in Iris's kitchen next to the back stairs across from the refrigerator.

"I miss those women already. They sure are fun," C.W. says.

"Yeah, I'm sure they're probably feeling the same about you," Eugene says, beating out a little rhythm on his thighs with his hands—rhythm, rhythm, rhythm.

"All right," Iris says. "That's enough. I don't want to hear any more. I'm going to go inside now."

"But you still get off on us, don't you, Mom?" C.W. says, elbowing over at Iris and then flashing her and Eugene both one of his biggest, most professional grins. "You love all the excitement of us, don't you, Mom? Me coming and me going.

You never know what next. You can't even guess what next. It keeps her young, Eugene."

"Well, to tell you the truth," Iris says, looking all around her at the dogs lying all around, then out at her zinnia bed, "I'd probably rather be somewhere else doing something else myself."

"Get out of here!" C.W. shrieks.

"Yes, I would."

The French Peugeot glimmers from the driveway under a streetlight. Iris takes a deep drag on her cigarette, kind of smiling.

"But I haven't so far thought of anything," she says, exhaling a long curling streamer of smoke. "And anyway, boys, somebody's got to be sitting on this porch smoking these goddamn Camels. Might as well be me so I can see what's what."

Angels

This day is the sweetest day. Other days you have to maybe tear up the place to find the bliss that this day has, its arms stretched out ready with warmth to jacket around thin shoulders, all right under Phoebe's nose, right under Phoebe's window, with her lying thin-shouldered and rolled up in a shivering ball in the upstairs bed.

This day speaks to Vernon, though—and he listens, he thinks about things. Vernon, who has his large self artfully arranged in a light sunshower on the front steps of Phoebe's house—right under Phoebe's nose, right under Phoebe's window—spooning up some yogurt with Phoebe's one angel-wing spoon, raindrops making sequins on his little cap of hair.

This day, it is morning still, Vernon is doing his work-break thinking on Phoebe's wooden steps, steps that would have to be worked on at some point, he can see that, as there are chips and dissolving parts rotting in the corners and nutty bugs with see-through wings that fly up and stick in his eyes.

The house looks bad, the steps look bad, but the day seems to have something good in it, something almost healing in it, and Vernon is thinking he might go inside if Phoebe does not show herself soon or make herself known like she does by crashing around in the kitchen. Vernon might go upstairs and hustle her sweet prissiness out of bed and prop her out here with him so she can get some of what he is getting from this amazing day. He can almost actually do something like that with Phoebe now. They might actually be mixed up with each other enough for him to knock on her door and make a simple suggestion.

Vernon has learned all the neighborhood sounds. There are decibels loaded with meaning. Things rumble, some only under his feet. Vernon can, more often than not, tell what is coming down the block blocks before he can actually see it. His very bones are re-tuned now from the previous house where he was working before. His bones are tuned up and working for this falling-down house where if Phoebe were really smart, if she had half an inspiration, she would just toss a match in and walk out, pulling shut the door.

The dog is selective. The dog barks, but not always. Sometimes the dog lets things come down the street and right up the driveway to the house and stays quiet while staring point-blank out the window. The part of the dog's routine that is a routine goes like this: The dog barks at the mailman but not at the laundry man. He barks at the UPS truck but not at the Chemlawn Service. And always, you can bet on it, the dog is apoplectic at the garbage men, who come up the driveway like a SWAT team.

The dog does not bark at Vernon anymore—maybe a couple of woofs. And after Vernon and the Chemlawn and the UPS people and the rest of them that are predictable entities, all dog routine is tossed out the window. What the dog does is a matter of the dog's mood or of how good he has been sleeping or if one of the cats has been giving him a hard time or if the position the moon was in, in the night sky, let moonlight fall across the house at an evil slant.

Vernon has gotten so he just lets himself in in the mornings, Phoebe staying in her room with the talk shows before showing herself girlish and waxy-skinned and smelling sickbeddish downstairs, her halter-top bandage looking faintly Grecian showing above where she wraps her robe with a sash. Phoebe doing what she has been doing lately: knocking things over going through the cabinets looking for coffee beans and filters or checking for cinnamon tea in the canisters beside the cooktop, all the noises Vernon has yet to hear this particular morning.

Vernon spends time musing on the spoon, turning it over and over in his hands, feeling its weight, rubbing the handle with his bent thumb where the angel wings are worked in silver. He balances the spoon on his knee and it rocks there slightly while he is rocking the top off a second carton of yogurt. He digs his hands into a bag of raisins and rains some down, spilling them out his cupped hand over the yogurt before doing some movement, smiling to himself and doing something vaguely priestlike with the silver spoon.

Phoebe is standing behind him. He senses her now, and looking back, he sees her, her face up close to the screen of the screened-in front porch looking veiled, a face barely there. Vernon's beginning to know Phoebe's presence before he knows she is there.

"You sitting out there in the rain for any reason, Vernon?" Phoebe says, holding an empty Limoges cup, the cup an old wedding present from her gone marriage like the spoon.

Vernon will get around to telling her to throw out all the plastic ones, the dumb mugs with the cleaners' names, the banks' names, stuff she has no business with now. "The sun is out too, you know, Phoebe," Vernon says. "Come on. You sit down here beside me and feel Nature's sauna. I have to wait for the plaster to set up."

"Somebody might see me in this robe," Phoebe says, looking up and down the block. "And I have to stay inside for the water to boil to make coffee. You want some?"

"So let them see you then," Vernon says. "You need to sit and let the sun melt some of that crust off, darlin'."

Going back inside, Phoebe starts upstairs for something for her hair while holding the robe up in her fist off from tangling in her ankles. Sighing so she can hear him, Vernon follows inside and busies himself with rinsing the spoon at the kitchen sink and with wiping it in a paper towel to lay it out on the countertop for Phoebe to use, it being the only piece of silver she will get out, the silver too beautiful for anything crazy— such as using it. Vernon tosses the empty yogurt cups in the garbage and dries his hands, thinking that given what life can be, some things are a blessed shame. Given what life can be, you better get out your whole silver service if you got it.

Vernon is plastering in the dining room, so he would have to be deaf not to hear the crashes—Phoebe, her hair in a thin ponytail, standing in the kitchen pulling down coffee beans and other things from the top shelf, opening and closing the refrigerator, talking to the animals while she opens a can of cat food for the cats, pours some dry dog food into the dog's dish, grinds up coffee beans for herself, and slams her way around, busy in a way that makes Vernon gradually begin to forget about her altogether, his mind coming back to his own drifting

thinking, such as to when he can find time to work on the
steps.

"Were you in my room?" Phoebe says. "I kept dreaming
you were in my room," she says, leaning up against the door
to the dining room, her arms crossed over her chest, and holding now a full cup of coffee in the Limoges cup.

Vernon is mixing up another bucket of plaster with a long
pine stick, turning the stick mostly two-handed and sometimes
making a little flipping move with one hand, flipping the tiny
Louis Vuitton purse he wears over his shoulder to his back
again and again but never taking it off. "Nope. Thought you
should be getting up, but no, I wasn't coming in to see if you
were still breathing."

"How can you call yourself a construction worker when
you wear that stupid purse?" Phoebe says.

"Sweetheart," Vernon says, "Phoebe, sweetheart, maybe we
do ourselves a favor by not calling some things anything." She
smiles for a moment. "Anyway," he says, dropping the stick
into the bucket and executing a sweeping turn, "I am not a
construction worker. What I choose to call myself in my real
life is an actor. This is not my real life." Then he walks from
one end of the dining room to the other and circles back again.
"I could teach you to model," he says. "You are thin enough
and have a look. It would give you the most fabulous life,
Phoebe, the life of being a model. If I weren't such a pig, I
would do it. If I weren't such a pig."

Suddenly, surprising Vernon even, Phoebe slips her hand in
his and pulls him through the house, Vernon jabbering, "Now
what in the world are you going to do with me? Just what?"
She pulls him back to the steps, where he crumples into a
slouch again, his purse dangling off his chest as she is stepping

her narrow body over his, which, in the skirts of her robe, Vernon sees flashing past his head, her toes bright with polish from some night of TV. Phoebe crawls herself headfirst on her hands and knees into the wild part of the yard, where the shrubs and plants and little trees and brush are woodsy and left strictly off-limits to any lawn-care efforts.

She fits herself back in with the bushes and says to Vernon, who adjusts his body slightly to see her better, "Tell me something, Vernon. What ever happened to the simple man in the paneled truck? Where's the handyman with his box of tools who does his work and just sends the bill?"

"Oh. Okay. I'm getting it," Vernon says. "I'm understanding you now," he says, lolling his head around and loosening up his neck, little flying bugs fanning out around the back of his head. "Well, just remember this, sweet pea. Remember this—you called me. I didn't call you. So come on and at least stick your legs out in the sun."

Phoebe sits up on one ankle, crossing the other leg over her knee, and folds herself into a Buddha shape deep in the brush. "I hate every minute. Every minute," she says.

Vernon shrugs. "Okay. Fine. Stay out of the sun. Sun's bad for your skin. Everybody needs good skin," he says. "I need good skin," he says to himself, fumbling in his breast pocket for a pair of sunglasses while Phoebe rolls this way and rolls that way, looking around on the ground to see if she is sitting on anything besides leaves and weeds and dirt, something like maybe a slug. Finally, she straightens up and sits quietly picking things off the palms of her hands.

Vernon watches for a while, then stares off down the block to where he had felt the mail truck was going to be coming up over the horizon pretty soon, and now the mail truck is actually doing it; coming; now stopping, right a few blocks up on Phoebe's street.

Phoebe and Vernon wait.

The dog climbs the front steps and scratches to get into the house. A station wagon goes by and hands trill out the windows. A bumblebee powers around the planter box as Phoebe and Vernon wait, gently lulled into that morning lull where the mail is on its way. Phoebe and Vernon wait, in a lull, for the mailperson who is not there, not there, not there—then is there, is here! suddenly, is all at once finally in view, the mailperson dressed in summer shorts and traipsing, kind of dancing down the block, working her way from house to house.

Vernon calls out to Phoebe. "Crawl on out here, Phoebs. Here comes some more get-well cards and your new *Rolling Stone.*"

The mailperson makes her way up Phoebe's front lawn, shifting her mailbag from one shoulder to the other while Vernon fidgets with getting his purse squared with his belt buckle, while Phoebe is stepping her way barefooted back deeper into the bushes, her robe gathered up in a wad in her lap.

The mailperson stomps one hiking boot up on Vernon's step, then does a thing to get her hair up out of her face. She pulls earphones from her ears and gives Vernon a grin.

Vernon glances over at Phoebe, who has a cat stepping over her lap going one way, then turning around and stepping over her going the other way.

The mailperson kisses towards Vernon with glossed lips, so Vernon kisses the air back at her. She digs out the mail and hands it to Vernon, so Vernon kisses the air at her again. Still grinning, the mailperson fixes her earphones back in her ears and goes off down the yard in the same way as she came, dancing, sort of gangly, slinging her bag back up on her shoulders on her way toward the neighbors'.

"She is leaving now, Phoebe," Vernon says, standing himself up on his feet.

Phoebe unfolds out of the bushes, the cat plunging down off across the yard.

"Some things are really an experience," Vernon says, wondering off after the mailperson, with Phoebe musing too. "Some things just knock me out."

This day later, early afternoon, Vernon's van, with Vernon driving Phoebe, is going along silhouetted against the sweetest, smoothest sky. When he hits city traffic, Vernon drives his van coasting and gunning and keeping to the slow lane, mostly staying trapped behind a city bus, even stopping when the bus stops and going when the bus goes. Coke bottles roll back and forth on the floorboards. Candy wrappers are wadded on the seats. Phoebe, in an old slidy raincoat somebody left in the front-hall closet, is kept from going through the windshield by the seat belt Vernon let loose as far as it would go and strapped over her balled-up body.

"Man," Phoebe says, heaving sighs.

Vernon is playing the tape he just bought on the tape deck and is beating on the dashboard, leaning forward from time to time to punch either the fast forward or the rewind.

Phoebe shakes her head.

"So, your-highness-queen-of-the-universe, what do you think?" Vernon says. "Good tunes? Whew! I like."

Phoebe looks out the window.

"Oh. Okay. I get it. You want me to go up there with you? I will go up there with you. Do you want me to?"

The road ahead opens up. The bus turns off. Vernon begins working his way through traffic, coasting a little, then gunning, then coasting, then gunning again to arc too widely around several cars and an ambulette, next double-parking in a towaway zone in the front of the professional building in the middle of the huge city hospital complex. Phoebe climbs down out of the van and stands looking back at Vernon through the open window.

"Okay now, Phoebe," Vernon says, "Listen here, Phoebe. This audition will take about two minutes for them to throw me out on my butt, so then I will come back here and wait right here out on the street for you. Right here this way or down there that way, but I'll try for here, so when you come out, be sure and look both ways, you know, both up and back down that way. I can't say what the parking situation will be when I get back here. By then."

"We deserve better," Phoebe says, Vernon nodding solemnly and saying, "Baby, baby, baby. Yes indeed, baby." Then Phoebe turns and goes up the walk.

Later on this blessed day, as early afternoon becomes real afternoon, no more lulls like with the mail, Vernon is parked out in the van doing breathing exercises. He does stints of holding his breath and raising up so he can look out the window to search the faces paddleboarding through the revolving door, a thing that makes him headachy, so he gives up on his exercises and picks up an old parking ticket to read that has been dropped with the bottles on the floorboards. He thinks about the lunch wagon he saw parked just around the corner and thinks about dashing over there for a bite. But there is always the chance that Phoebe might paddleboard herself out of the professional building and forget how she ever got where she is and wander off to get herself a taxi home.

.   .   .

"I am here to tell you that there are many, many things that can hurt," Phoebe says to Vernon through the window as she is trying to work the door handle.

Vernon jerks his head up, his arm resting on the back of the seat. "Hold on. Let me get that," he says, springing into action.

"Let's trade places, Vernon," Phoebe says, getting in the van. "I got to drive. You have to let me drive because I need to have something to do with myself right now. I have to run this one last lousy errand."

Shifting her over by sliding her across on top of him, Vernon says, "Phoebe, believe me. Phoebe, from the bottom of my heart. We all go through things. We all of us go through things."

In the parking lot of the department store where Phoebe has her errand, she stands shoving up and dropping down the sleeves of her raincoat while Vernon circles around locking up the van. He buckles his knees to spit-shine away a dirt spot that turns out to be a door chip.

As they go in through the cosmetics department, silvered tree branches arc over their heads and there are lead crystal vases filled with peacock feathers sitting on the glass counters. Vernon hypers around trying to find the escalator, to find the store directory, while Phoebe moves slower, moves along peacefully browsing the counters. She stops to rub an anti-aging lotion on the back of her hand and to watch a how-to makeup videotape. She takes a perfume sample from a pretty woman in a cocktail dress holding a little hill of them on a tray.

Vernon spots a sign offering a gift box of candy just for today, just for opening a store charge account. He wanders nearby to the little gilded desk manned by a charge-account man and digs out his driver's license and a couple of credit cards. He reaches for a pen. As Vernon glances over at Phoebe, which he does from time to time, he sees that she is mostly just working her way along the counters messing with testers or looking at what's in a free-gift-with-purchase package. Later, when he glances at her, he sees something new; he sees Phoebe locked in a gaze with herself in a mirror, one finger raised, barely touching her face. And with her free hand, she is raking her nails through her wind-knotty hair.

Vernon reaches for the box of candy and goes to Phoebe, slipping his arms around her from the back. Then he takes Phoebe and walks her, the two of them together, to a counter with more of everything, with the unusual as well as the usual, with tiny bottles of glitter suspended in clear gels and a vivid bank of testers stair-stepping up next to a column tied with the silvered tree branches.

"Okay," he says to her, flipping his purse over his shoulder. "Hold still and I will do you. Yes?"

Vernon works loose Phoebe's top button and in soft, loose folds drops the slippery raincoat down off her shoulders. He uses his thumbnail to break the cellophane on the box of candies, then hands them back to Phoebe. "Here is lunch, sweetness," he says to her as she begins to settle nicely under the pressure of his hands cleaning her face with astringent-soaked cotton balls.

Then picking up a piece of candy from the box, Vernon crushes it slightly, then puts it back, then picks up another and crushes it, and then finally he feeds one to Phoebe and eats several himself. "This is nice," Phoebe says, searching around in the box. Vernon puts his hands on her head and holds her still, bringing her face up so he can stare intently into her eyes. "Okay. I got it," he says.

Rubbing a cream into her damp skin, he says, "SPF of 15. Always use an SPF of 15. But then you already know that. I don't have to tell you that. Jesus. I need to tell myself that."

He reaches for a small sponge and next works in a pale foundation, one shade lighter than Phoebe's skin. He fluffs her face with fine-milled rice powder and buffs the powder, bringing her face up to a satin finish. Standing back, he studies her for a moment, crossing his legs at the ankles and looking in the mirror and back at Phoebe, going back and forth, Phoebe moving her face to the mirror and back along with him.

Vernon then studies the candy box for a moment. Brown pleated candy wrappers are scattered all over the counter. He collects himself up, sighing, choosing a small brush, and starts in on Phoebe's eyes, first brushing her brows up with a little dark powder; then using his fingers, the brush, and the fat part of his thumb, Vernon works a whole palette around her eyes, using colors in a layering fashion, some matte colors, some metallic colors, some just no color, just brown and just almond, these shades all going up to her brow and spreading out from the corners of her eyes.

"You okay?" Phoebe asks.

"Me?" he says, pausing to push back a few loose dangles of her hair. "Me? I am the handyman. Of course I am okay."

"Well, I, for one, dare I say it? I am having fun," Phoebe says. "I love the chocolates. This is all very nice, Vernon. Very sweet."

"Well, look at you, Phoebe-bean! Angel-wing eyes, for God's sake. And having fun too. Listen. Tell me something, sweetness. And tell me true. Do I look old or what?" he says, bringing his face up close to Phoebe's and leaning his shoulder into the curve of her bare shoulder. "This part's serious."

"You look good, Vernon," she says, beginning to fidget, getting her arms high enough to hold him off. "Sort of youngish. Medium-young old."

"Everything I want you have to be young for," he says, returning upright.

"Everything I want you have to get old for," Phoebe says, leaning around to see herself in the mirror.

"Well, what do you think of that? We should trade then," Vernon says, pulling her raincoat up from around her shoulders, and shaking it up in little shakes to glide evenly over her shoulders. He kisses her on the top of her head, smelling her hair with the kiss, and twirls away from her, saying, "Okay, Phoebe McPhoeb, I only care about the eyes. You do your lipstick any way or no way at all."

He begins to put some color on his own face, to edge his own eyes with a fine pencil line. "God! Jesus, I just am seeing myself," he says. "Well, do as I say and not as I do, baby-cakes, you know—about the sun."

Phoebe busies herself with testers, running colors across the back of her hand. She picks out a screaming bright color for her lips. "Now I want to buy all this stuff," she says to Vernon. "Now I have to own all this stuff."

"Oh, good God no, certainly not, heavens no. Absolutely not," Vernon says. "That is what the Walgreen's is for. You ever go to the Walgreen's? The shampoo aisle alone—"

"How do I look?" Phoebe says, slipping off the chair and turning toward him.

Vernon walks a few steps away from the counter, then comes back and picks up the chocolates. He works at fitting the top back on the box, but the little pleated papers are springy and will not go flat.

"How do I look?" Phoebe says.

Vernon looks over at her and heaves a sigh. He offers out his arm for her to fold into, her standing there not moving, her arms hanging at her sides, the raincoat skimming her body.

"I am exhausted, Phoebe," he says, heaving another, even deeper sigh. "So let's go find the tit lady and get this thing over with."

. . .

They wander aisles, ride the escalator, make a stop by the drinking fountain while working their way back to the lingerie department, even at one point going back past the charge-account man, who lifts another box of candy at Vernon. "Oh, tit lády, oh, tit lady," Vernon calls. They work their way back to where there are racks and racks of nightgowns and robes, camisoles and other underthings, Vernon nudging Phoebe along, her saying in different ways the same thing, Phoebe saying, "Oh, this is just beautiful. That was a wonderful way to put it, Vernon. I am just loving every bit of this myself. Come on. Leave. Go. Let me go alone."

Vernon keeps the two of them going, steering Phoebe along by keeping one of his hands firmly on the back of her neck, all the while with the other hand fingering the different materials that they use for these kinds of things, flipping his fingers through fragile laces that stir around, that ruffle a bit, and then blowing on other things that puff sleepily up in the air and then drift back down before sighing into silken folds. "No way. I'm seeing this thing through to the end."

Phoebe says, "Whatever *did* happen to the old days when the handyman arrived in a paneled truck and then left and sent the bill? What *did* happen to the nice fellow who got himself up from J. C. Penney? Now we have designer purses. Now we have involvement."

"Listen, Phoebe," Vernon says, "Give me your hand! Give me your hand! Listen to me, Phoebe. There's not all that much involvement. I am doing your house, and when your house is done or when you run out of money or when I get bored out of my skull, whichever comes first, then I'm doing somebody else's house. That's still the bottom line, just like in the old days with the paneled truck."

Vernon dips close to a freestanding designer trunk-show rack of drippy chiffon. "It's all about money, chimichanga," he says, maneuvering his head so something mistlike is passing over his forehead. "And when I get my shit together, then I'm doing nobody's house—would that that day would ever come, oh God, please, come, come."

Phoebe, seeing him veiled in this way, smiles and juts up a shoulder, which nudges him so he stumbles, having to grab hold of the rack and step clear through to the other side to keep his balance, all the while dragging her along behind him. Gowns that slip easily off their hangers are drifting to the floor, and Phoebe and Vernon, anxious with trying not to get their makeup on something, with not pulling the whole rack down on top of them, anxious with trying to keep upright while all the while they are falling with the utmost of care that they can muster and even some grace, Phoebe and Vernon fall along with the gowns and negligees and peignoirs and bed jackets, all of them top-of-the-line designer-expensive, all of them strewing around with Phoebe and Vernon, all of them going down on the floor rumpling up together.

Vernon sighs and gently lies flat down on his back on the store linoleum squares and stretches out his arm for Phoebe to rest her head on. From the things still hanging, delicate creamy laces stream a muted light and glowing satin ribbons loop and trail into soft folds on the floor.

Vernon looks up at the pipes on the ceiling and Phoebe watches feet walking up and down out in the aisle.

"Oh my God," Phoebe says.

"Just use some old socks. Forget the lady. We'll get you a whole pack of sweat socks at the Walgreen's. Just stuff them in something, you know."

"Where is the candy box," says Phoebe. "And will you please quit saying 'tit lady,' Vernon, you faggot."

"I did not this time say 'tit lady.' You are just reacting all on your own as if I did, and also I cannot even look at you eating those things anymore," Vernon says, shoving the candy box out into the middle of the aisle.

Phoebe rolls over on her stomach and looks in Vernon's face.

"Angel-wing eyes," he says. "I am a hell of an artist, Phoebe. Look at you! Actually, you look like hell. Just kidding."

Phoebe reaches up behind his head and checks the price tag of a gown lying on the floor. "You look worse than me. Just kidding. No I'm not."

"Phoebe, sometimes I get the strangest feeling. Sometimes I get the feeling you are giving me your death."

"Hear that, God? Vernon is volunteering the ultimate. What a guy."

Vernon adjusts his arm a little and looks up at the pipes on the ceiling. "The sleaziest, the very sleaziest—"

"Well, I guess you could just add it to your bill, couldn't you, Vernon." she says. "Like with the paneled truck? But I think you have your life and your death and I have mine and that the two don't have a thing to do with each other. Not one thing. Wish they did. Wish they did."

"Okay, well, are we having fun yet? That is the thing," Vernon says, rubbing Phoebe's back since both his arms are wrapped around her, with her relaxing on top of him and dangling her arms down off his sides. "What are we going to do? What are we going to do, baby, baby?"

More people walk up and down out in the aisle. A lingerie lady comes and begins adjusting the rack, Phoebe and Vernon lying silent on the other side. Soon the lingerie lady goes away, calling out for some woman named Ethel. "Ethel, Ethel," she says.

"Go to the Walgreen's?" Phoebe says, unfolding herself and beginning to untangle her arms and legs from Vernon and disentangle herself from a bunch of silky things. She starts to get up off the floor.

And Vernon, standing up along with her and working his way free of a peignoir, then getting his purse untangled from where the strap was close to strangling him, says, "Well then, give me your hand, Phoebe, and we'll go where we can get us a better deal on body parts."

"Not here," Phoebe says. "You sure not here?"

"And show some dignity getting out of this place, girl," Vernon says.

"You really dying for me, Vernon? Hey, Ethel, he's mad for me, he's practically dying for me."

"Shut up. Walk, Phoebe," Vernon says. "Come on, just hold my hand you little tarted-up—"

"Angel," Phoebe says.

Licensed for Private Exhibition Only

Now me—no matter what it is I do, to me he says, "Oh, what are you doing that for?" No matter what! Could be ice chips, how full I fill the cups, or the cuticle on his finger I pick at too long or too hard. Also, maybe something I drag over from home for him is not now in a pleasing shade.

Her, he picks up the phone on his bedside and says, "Hey, let me have your Boston cream pie slice. If you don't want it."

I say, "What are you doing that for?" and jerk on his fingers, and he says, "Tina, what are you doing that for?" about me, and into the phone he says, "Coppertone, we are coming over *en entourage!*"—him from his cranked-up bed, the sheet dipping between his bent-up knees.

He is pushing back the tray table and is fighting off the sheet and has got one leg dangling over the side of the bed already and hangs up the phone wrong, and I am seeing his ankle, and it is starting me to thinking this crazy thing about how his ankle is in the factual window daylight; it is like nothing that suits him, with a black hair here and there, sprouting here and there, like something struggling to grow up in a rock crack and not doing too well, and I am thinking of how he looks to be riding his motorcycle, his hair styled wind-slicked-back, every hair scraped back by force and then going crazy out the back like flames licking air and sunlight, like joy even. I start to wondering things and then think the thing that is important: that he does not call me Tina, he calls me Moonface is my name, and now with her Coppertone, I am Tina again.

"Grab that bottle of wine there, Tina, okay?" he says.

Boredom is what I tell myself I feel. We are there, him knocking on the doorframe in a little rhythm, leaning forward some in the chair from eagerness and from what must be pain too, me behind using my weight, pushing and trying to steer him around the sharp turn into her corner room, jerking the chair an inch or two to get him lined up so we go in straight and don't bang and scrape metal on wood.

This lady in there clicks off the TV and pulls the little chain on her reading light and looks up at the two of us. She is a blond person with short curly hair, big shoulders and jaw.

"Hi, Troy. Is this her?" she says, and she smiles, using muscles in her face I never thought to even think about.

I say, "Hey," to this woman, and my hand waves itself at her, nothing planned.

Her bed is a messy place, a longtime home for a person, like the dogs' beds get sometimes when they just sleep there night after night, year after year, and things are ground in. Her bed is not that bad, but my mind does do an easy goose step to the dogs' beds because her sheets are rumpled and there is a coffee spill and it does not look like this morning's coffee either. Her own flowered pillowcase from home must be on one of her pillows, a pillowcase with turquoise and red flowers, Hawaiian-looking, orchidy things, full-blown, noisy flowers with wide-open mouths, the whole thing soon surely ready for a run-through in the Maytag, but the right person has not noticed this, and it will not be me doing the pointing out. Also, there are catalogues lying around on the covers, so I guess she has been ordering things for herself or doing her Christmas shopping early, I am to suppose. And on her table tray is a slice of the pie he wants, and alongside it there is a clean fork.

He is buggy, trying to get me to get his chair in some right place he has in his mind without taking his eyes off the woman in the bed, and I finally get him where he wants to be, and he rests his foot up on the metal bed frame like it is what he always does, you know, like sidling up to someplace, maybe a bar, and fine, so I settle in the vinyl armchair off to the side and pull my legs up under me and cross my arms hard and listen to things myself in my own head that will help me, and I calm down like this.

"I am going on a safari to Kenya," Coppertone says, "when I get out of here."

Neither of us, Troy or me, says one thing to that, so after a while she shrugs and calls down to the nurse on the speaker intercom asking for fresh ice, ice chips for the plastic pitcher sitting on her tray table, and Troy picks up the wine bottle and goes to work on it with a corkscrew he carried in here on himself. Maybe in his robe pocket. I think about getting up and that I could be lining up three Styrofoam cups on the metal chest of drawers and decide that I will when I want to be doing something. He is still fixing the wine bottle anyway. The ice comes, and so I get up and grind some cups upside down, which works good enough to fill them, and they will be kind of wine slushes, I am thinking, so I tear the top off the paper on a bendy straw and accordion it down and blow the accordion paper toward the cool, pine-smelling, chromy bathroom, where something of hers pink and nylon is hung up on a hanger on the shower rod. I cannot see it too well, so I am only guessing at what it is, but I am a woman who rinses out things and my guesses are good. The bendy straws are what the nurse gave me from the pocket of her skirt when I asked her for some straws. The nurse is black, and her I do like a great deal, which is how I usually feel toward people, but some are exceptions, I am coming to know.

Lace smoke snippets, it looks to be, slipping out the side of her mouth, Coppertone's goddamned whip-cracking-out a match lighting up a filter cigarette. And next, she is polite and passing around the box of truffles her grandmother sent her; they are big, the size of golf balls, rolled first in cocoa powder and then in white powdered sugar, and they are special things. They make the wine taste sour, though, like the kids are hard on me saying orange juice tastes to them after they have eaten their pancakes and syrup first, exactly in the wrong order. But the wine is cold and nice, like a wine slush is supposed to be.

She is looking over at me sitting in the corner in the vinyl armchair where I am. My face feels good on my head, it just does is all. She sits there in her bed, staring up over her cup, her lips, her mouth still on the cup like she is drinking; her eyes she is lifting and looks at me, and I know this is something different for her, the way we are, Troy and I, or maybe just the way I am. The way we are is a couple, and she has only seen him as him, and the way I am is moon-faced, with my black hair, and that is something alongside his blond straight hair and chiseled upper lip and kind of pouting bottom lip and smartness, and we are a couple with children at home. My whole self says, "Yes, honey," at her without saying a word, and she hears me, I know she does, and so she turns away from me to where Troy is, anywhere where I am not.

She and Troy talk hospital talk, patient talk, about is there any sense to anything anyway, and tell each other how hard things are and how much they are in pain and what a time they are having.

Troy says, "I am going to get really well. I am going to get more well than Tina (me) over there. I might work in this hospital."

Coppertone nods. "I will never come back to this hospital, or any other, when I get out," she says.

I watch them through slits in my eyes, and they prism as if I am seeing them out of a fly's eyes.

"I know how old people feel now, so that is good," Coppertone says to somewhere off at the wall it looks like.

"That's right, we sure know that," Troy says.

Well, it could have waited, there is time, I think. It is nothing I am in a hurry to know, how old people feel, though what I say is "That is right, you do, and I don't," which is what they want to hear.

Troy says, "This pie is good. Here, Tina, have a taste," and turns around and looks at me hard because he knows how I feel on matters.

I hold up my hand with the truffle, which means no, and slit my eyes at them again, all around the room slitted, into the bathroom, all around the room into places they do not even know about in this room.

"I think I was put in here for a reason," Troy says to Coppertone, forgetting about me and getting to what he always gets to. I can hear it coming, that God did it to him for a reason, that God selected him out and flung him around His head like he was a rock on the end of a rope because he was not living the best life. God was on to him.

I say, "Well, you are going to be out of here faster than you can say Jack Rabbit," is what I say and push my skirt up to look at my knees.

Neither of them says anything, but there is something in the air, and Coppertone passes Troy the last cigarette from her soft pack as she smiles a small smile and says to me, "Honey? Call down to the nurses' station and tell them it is time for my medication, would you be such a darling?"

I heave myself out of the armchair, untangling my arms and legs, setting the rest of the truffle I ate only part of on her bedside table. "I will just walk," I say, hanging myself with my arm like a gate hinge on the back of Troy's chair, then swinging around his neck to give him a kiss.

The nurse follows me in, carrying tiny paper pill cups and two evil hypodermics on a tray, and there they are, Troy and Coppertone, smoking up the room, and her now, both hands in the bedside-table drawer, pawing through VHS cassettes, cigarette sticking straight out her mouth, eyes squinted up like mine are when I am doing fly eyes. Troy is laughing and looks to be in a slingshot, slung back low like he is in his wheelchair, blowing smoke rings high in the room, roping dead patient spirits and reading cassette warnings out loud off videocassettes. But he is doing one smart thing: his legs he has up on her bed now to move the blood in a different direction so it does not pool in his ankles and make clots and kill him and end this whole thing.

I look around the room with eyes that feel bigger and bigger, as *swoosh!* the nurse opens the window wide, which slides up like on air, sucking the smoke out of the room like the thing above my stove at home, some machine somewhere out there in the night just turned on, and I stand back a minute to watch, and it is something, it is working, and I am thinking about the smoke sucked out of that room like one huge spirit now with smoke ropes fraying fast around its neck, now here with us, now choking us and causing sickness, then just gone. Just not here. I stare with big eyes at the easiness of it, then catch myself as the nurse bumps me while moving around the foot of the bed, and so I grab for the ashtrays to be dumping them out and tidying up, rinsing them with cold bathroom water, smiling new and wide at the nurse as she nurses Troy and Coppertone since their medication schedules are the same. I splash some wine in our chewed-up, tooth-marked cups where it has been drunk low, offer around what truffles are left, and in the bathroom I put on some pearl lipstick I find lying out there on the basin and comb my hair up in a tight twist with tap water and stick in a few bobby pins I dig out of my tote. My wet hands I roll in the hem of her nightgown hanging up there on the shower rod until they are as dry as nylon can get anything that is wet, all the time thinking that the room is cleaned up now and nothing is the same and things will get better. When I come out of the bathroom, I feel new and good and clean and say, "Come on, you all! Let's get well in here!" and I clap my hands a couple of times.

Where they had their shots they rub themselves with hands made tight into fists and look over at me, electrified and standing in the bathroom high-watt light, and I am a thing to make them blink huge, slow blinks that take time. Then one of them says, "Come on," to the other, "I guess we should brush our teeth or something."

"My teeth are fine," the other one says, and that is the end of that, as I know they are slipping back down into their sickness, where they want to be, no matter what, so . . .

Fine.

Fixing my lipstick with my finger, I get behind Troy and lean forward and say, to be trying, because I am his wife, "Let us go on back to your room now, honey, okay? That shot is going to be working and you can sleep. You don't want to be staying up all night looking at some dumb movie." Troy does not say anything to me, so I go over to the woman's bed and start looking through her catalogues and asking her about the things in them she likes. Her shot is working and she is nicer.

Coppertone says, "Look here, Tina. Look at this nightgown and robe I ordered. Just put it on my Visa card."

I look.

"Now, what have you done with your hair, Tina?" Troy says, leaning sideways and back in his chair, holding his cigarette out away from him, up-handed.

"I just pushed it up and stuck some pins in it. Nothing."

"Oh," he says and is gone, I know, because I am watching for it. I get back in my armchair, toes hooking over his wheel spokes, and we get into more wine, and they start talking and banging VHS cassettes until they decide to screen one even though it is late, a weird movie set in Texas Troy shows over and over at home. I only hate it more every time I see it is all I can say about this movie. I curl in on myself, my knees tight up against my chest, my back curling like something fitted snug in a shell just opened enough to see out of, and it is like this that I nod through the credits, then sleep like a baby halfway through the movie until I wake with Troy shaking my shoulder: "Help me, Tina. I got to lie flat, help me get in there with Coppertone until the movie is over."

We clear off the catalogues and put the movie on pause, and Coppertone moves over to the side closer to the radiator, and I help Troy and straighten out his legs and get his back fixed up flat and find a pillow and stuff it up under his knees. I even get extra pillows from his room next door and put them where he says he wants them—it is an ordeal—and I fix Coppertone up with some cream she wants for her hands and the lip gloss for her lips, which are cracking, and I settle them in like babies—but easier than the boys at home, who always kick and never need a thing like sleep and quiet, and who wake each other up if one of them ever does make it to sleep. These two are easy to settle. I go in Coppertone's bathroom and run a washcloth over my face, then climb back in the vinyl armchair, the movie flickering in the pitch-black room, Coppertone and Troy in her little hospital bed cranked up just a little for both of them, Coppertone and him in her bed making two red cigarette eyes like a crazy thing that kind of scares me if I look at it too long, smoke breath making quick for the window, no sound from the movie, as it is too late in the night for sounds that are not screams or snores or moans or something crackling in on the intercom.

Coming close to sleep, my mind moves around thoughts better left alone I truly believe.

So I think about how we got into this place, what happened, which is wonder enough and easy. Easy as being worn out, which is what he was. He was tired is all. Nothing happened. It was just his way of taking his leave on things that have gotten hard, his way of saying he needs a rest or maybe needs a change is what it is. It is his surprisedness at the hardness that I do not understand, as I am not surprised by much and everything seems hard anyway. He is the one who brings up God, about being at the end of God's rope is the way it seemed for him, God twirling him around His head is how he came to be skidding in that beautiful arc, a slid arc, a gorgeous arc that went on and on across black almost-liquid-boiled-up asphalt, goldenrod and ragweed bunching up on each side of the road, smearing the only colors there were that he saw and remembered. God's colors. Golds like the sun.

So far, thank God, God does not have me at the end of some rope knocking my brains out and breaking all my bones and cooking me up in boiling asphalt. He is giving me a chance here to be quiet is how I see it.

I am happy. There are truffles to bite into, to see what is in the middle, and apple juice if I want to go down the hall for it. I can sip my wine as slow as I want, pull pins out of my hair, drop them each one on the floor, and shake my hair loose, maybe dance a little, rubbing my arm, dance alone in the dark to the movie music if I care to use the earphones. I can call the kids and see what they are up to, then climb back in the vinyl armchair, put my head down, and be sleeping curled up, my hair waterfalling like rapids over my crossed arm, and wait like that. Wait maybe for God's hand on my hair, which is the way He might come to me. I can sleep anywhere waiting for that. I just let it be hard while it is hard, without going crazy for it to get easy.

Powwow

The deadeye sun just ups and moves over, and this changes things; with the trees in the front yard staying put, not moving, and being no longer in the way, everything is cleared for the sun to slap light across Alma's spun-sugar hair, her blue-tinted hair, where Alma sits dialing the phone. She is calling up the girl, Avery.

And now Avery, she picks up at the kitchen extension in the house where she lives with all the children and all the boarders, and Alma, introducing herself, says to Avery, "I am Alma from the complex," but in a smart voice, not in an old-lady voice, a voice so smart that Avery thinks this must be another real estate lady calling, until this crazy thing is said, namely, until Alma says, "Avery? Marian—you know Marian—just hung herself and Popo cannot make a thing of anything."

"Who is Popo?" Avery says, though truthfully in a way mostly looking at her gauzy dog through the kitchen-door screen, the skinny dog bending himself around to get to something on his rear half with his tiny front teeth.

"Popo is your granddaddy, Avery. I am his friend. I am Alma from the complex."

"I never heard anyone call him Popo," Avery says.

"That is the name Marian gave him."

"Who is Marian?" Avery says. "Who is this Marian?"

"The old lady Marian. Your granddaddy's girlfriend Marian. The half-breed lady Marian."

"Is that what happened? She hung herself?" says Avery.

"Avery. I am trying to tell you these things. I am just one of your granddaddy's friends," Alma says, sounding worn out to Avery all of a sudden.

"Popo?" Avery says.

"It's the only name your granddaddy will answer to. And hey, listen," Alma says. "Popo is set back with this thing and all I hear him talking about now is family, hear?"

No matter. At this point, Avery herself is frankly worn down a notch or two by the flow of life, and not knowing what is what anyway, she is actually ready to pull up the slack some and come across the state line for a visit, to see the granddaddy she remembers mostly for his bad temper and the ice-cream plant he built up from nothing that seemed to cause the bad temper, and not as much for the Cherokee blood, which was the main thing when she was a kid. She is ready to see him in his retirement condominium, where she has heard there are old ladies and romance. Avery has heard these things in letters and vaguely of Alma too and of Marian in these letters, and so, leaving her three children in the good hands of her boarders, some of these boarders even living just behind screens that partition off sections of the huge house, like the screen decorated with a heron standing on one foot in the living room and another screen painted with flaking Chinese red and age-deepened gold fencing off an alcove on the third floor, Avery packs up some things in a beat-up leather bag, borrows the big car with air conditioning, and goes to Popo, her granddaddy, with the idea of a powwow lighting on her spirit and rising like a bubble in her heart.

Back at Avery's, there is no man there now on a permanent basis but for the boarders—some of them are men. And Avery is just now coming to an age—to the other side of life, the darker side—where she feels some things are gone and others are not the same, and something in her has the common sense to want and yearn for what is slipping away.

And now here comes Avery in the big loaded car she has borrowed, her hair sliding around and across her shoulders, driving through the tollbooth, tossing coins at the toll basket, and also now picking up the car phone and calling up Alma to say to Alma just where she is, she is at the tollbooth ten minutes away, "so start checking whatever it is you need to check, maybe the stove and the coffeepot, because we are rushing and—my fault entirely—we are running late."

Alma, twisting the fingers of her gloves, which lie across her lap like little kittens gone limp, with her scared to meet Avery and wanting Avery both (she is not Avery's mother, though she might be, would want to be), her chin lifts up with purpose as she is talking to Avery, and she says, softly now, into the phone, "I am bringing you here for your granddaddy. It's just something I have thought to do for him with what has happened."

Avery nods a wisp of a nod, the breath of a nod, and crawls her hand around inside her purse for some lipstick to slick her lips with. She says, "I hope somebody will just tell me what happened."

Alma is old and has skin so softened with fine-powder film that Avery is aroused to touch it with her finger when she meets Alma in person for the first time at the door of her studio apartment in the sprawling retirement condominium. She settles Alma in the back seat of the car, where Alma is a frilly thing, a dressing-table ornament with lacy cuffs that shiver like aspen leaves at her wrists, whose first conversation is not about death or hanging or love but about keeping the icebox cake she has put together in her little kitchenette from turning rancid in the furnace blast of this day. Avery thinks to turn the air-conditioning nozzles so they blow cold air all together at the round-cornered cake that Alma cradles so tenderly in her lap.

Avery starts up the car and Alma talks, and in her voice Avery is hearing the real estate lady again.

"You do not look like the trouble I heard you were, Avery," Alma says. "You are a nice-looking young woman."

"I am fat now," Avery says.

"You do not mean it. I would like to know where any fat is, you cute thing!" Alma says.

"Baby fat from the babies," Avery says, pulling her sleeve tight over her upper arm and holding it up to show it is bigger than it should be.

"We all have that!" Alma says.

"To me it is a new thing," Avery says, and neither of them says anything for a while, just thinking, as embarrassment rises gently between them, and Alma starts fussing with the cake, rotating the cake to check all sides.

"That poor woman, that Marian. I cannot imagine what went wrong with her," Alma says from some new mood.

"I never knew anyone who killed herself, so I cannot imagine being on either side of it," Avery says, putting the car in gear and driving off, swinging around the corner of the retirement condominium, a low pale brick building on golf-course-perfect grass dotted with little staked and roped young trees, humming with a sprinkler system, all this out in the middle of nowhere where only interstates connect. The two women sight Popo. They watch him emerge through an iridescent heat, hanging on to his chrome walker, a torch of bright gladiolas woven in through the bars. Popo, wearing a dark suit with floppy legs and mile-wide lapels and looking to Avery in his old age, with the fat padding gone between him and the world, more the Indian he is than ever.

His gladiolas lurch in a springy, fluid fashion with the walker as Popo makes his way, taking two straight-legged steps, then replacing the walker a bit ahead, and then taking two more steps and moving the walker again, the way life has left him to walk now. Small petals and bits of leaves shake loose, and they fall, leaving a little trail.

Sighting who he guesses is Avery, him being alerted to her coming, Popo shouts at her, "Oh, Avery, Avery, did you know about Marian? She is dead," as if they kept each other up with things, a practice they certainly have not done.

"Ohhh—your flowers," Avery says, standing by the car, and her thumb cannot find the strength to punch in the button to open the door for him, so Popo reaches over her and opens it himself and then, knees cracking, sits sideways in the seat and becomes absorbed with his walker, first thing pulling out the gladiolas and handing them over to Avery to hold and then collapsing the walker for her to fit in the trunk.

On seeing him again and up close, Avery gets the feeling things are beginning to change around in her, causing her emotions to mix up and to run together, her getting a firm handle on not one of them. And the sum total of this hodge-podge is to allow yearning to sneak in and to grab up a bigger fistful of her heart than it already has hold of and to hang on hard. That he is still a big-shouldered man with skin like clay dirt wrapped over carved cheekbones, and though now old, his skin is lined only in the way the skin on her palms is lined or the bottoms of her feet, there really are no wrinkles, and that at his shirt collar there is a string tie with a jawbreaker-sized chunk of turquoise for a pull, pale sunlit turquoise, a thing she would want to wear at her shirt collar, and that he combs his hair straight back and smooth are some of the reasons. And that her mama is dead.

"Avery, tell me. How are the children? Is everyone all right?" Popo says. "And how are you back there, Alma?" he says to Alma, twisting his whole body slightly but not all the way around to look at her.

Alma's eyes are like saucers looking at Popo from her vantage perch in the back seat with the cake, and this look is not lost on Avery as she walks back trancelike to the trunk of the car with the walker, carrying it over her arms in the manner she might carry long-stemmed roses should that occasion ever occur.

"I do not know what happened," Popo says, his eyes black and wide, turning back to Avery, who is now sliding herself under the steering wheel.

"You can never really know what goes on with another person, really," Alma says from the back seat. Avery looks in the rearview mirror at Alma, seeing her just in the shape of the mirror, just her eyes, which are kind of pretty done up as they are with pale colors in a way that brings to Avery's mind that odd stone they set in rings sometimes, the star sapphire, with its colors flung out from a washed-out moon in the middle.

Popo, waving his hand just from the elbow, locked at the

wrist, says, "Where did you get this fancy car, sister? You got a phone in here, and I do not know what all."

Avery looks over at her granddaddy, at Popo. He is now punching in the lighter, which will not stay punched in, and fumbling in his breast pocket, spilling papers and getting like all men she has known get—exasperated, fed up with things. He places the cigarette between his lips in a delicate way, the way a jeweler might set that stone, that star sapphire, Avery thinks, as she gets the lighter to work right for him; it was only a matter of not punching it so hard.

"Today is a shame, a crying shame," he says, moving his lips around the cigarette.

"Well, it is a terrible thing," Avery says.

"Oh, Avery, I do not know how I will ever get over the things that happen in this life," Popo says, finally lighting up and blowing out a roiling cloud of smoke to go slow, down around in the air-conditioned air.

"See, it is the living, not the dead, that are left with the mess, all the guilt," Alma says from the back seat, leaning her tinted head between the two of them. "And here we are, the living, just as they say."

"Where did Marian get that name for you? The name Popo?" Avery says.

Popo glances at her, then busies himself picking at his clothes and doodling with the cigarette and messing with the tiny ash and hitting it on the side of the ashtray and looking out the window spellbound by something out there. Avery squirms under his power, the power to ignore her, and Alma says things from the back seat that do not mean anything or fit in with the conversation, as she cannot hear well what they have been saying now that they are on the expressway and the air conditioning is turned up full.

Kind of surprising her, later, he says, "I came to like it."

Even later, he says, "Avery? Don't you remember the Popo Bar we used to make at the ice-cream factory? The thing dipped in butterscotch?"

From way up on the expressway bridge where they are, Avery drives them all past the funereal church, seeing it shimmering white down below, and she can hear, even with the windows rolled up and the air conditioning on, the gravel under the wheels of the cars that are slowly rolling into the small church parking lot, where there is a graveyard in back, stone and cement crosses sticking up here and there, not one of them straight up or coming out of the ground at the angle they were put in or the graves kept up as was somebody's plan.

Now, ramping down a cloverleaf like on a tilt-a-whirl, all of them flattened up against car doors or hanging on to something, Avery on automatic pilot, her being a mother, automatically sticks her hand out flat across Popo, and Alma crawls a hand up on his shoulder until the car has righted itself and all four wheels are back to bearing equal weight. Next, they dive-bomb straight down on the church like a chunk of ice coming down a chute as the church is exactly at the bottom of the straight final part of the cloverleaf ramp and their big car is fast.

While all three have their hands occupied working on the mysterious unlocking device on their seat belts, Popo mumbles something at Avery. He says, "You sure were a hellion, sister."

Inside the church, they make their way to the front like a single being, hooked together by arms. They place the gladiolas along with the other flowers on top of Marian's casket, and in the pew the two women work together folding up Popo's walker and laying it down flat where it clanks on the uneven wooden floor under their feet. Then Alma and Avery and Popo rest their shoes on top of it, using it to rest their feet.

There are people seated in the sanctuary, most of them near the front, thinning out toward the back to maybe one or two here or there. The service begins, and Popo thrusts his chin out goosenecked and holds it that way until the hymn singing, and when Avery pulls open her purse to look for offering money, a wad of thick Kleenex unfurls itself slightly like a surprise live thing somebody picked a rock up off of. She separates a Kleenex out and offers it to Popo, who takes it with a hand held down-handed and flat.

After the service, there is a reception across the pasture at a nearby farmhouse, a small frame house with forever aluminum siding with a picnic table and chairs scattered around a patio in back, a little place where people can sit and talk and have something cold to drink. Have something to eat. But just desserts. There is a table of wonderful desserts, all like Alma's icebox cake and every bit as good.

Under the afternoon sun that cannot touch them, tucked as they are safely under a broad-leafed tree over by a dried-out fence, is where Avery and Alma and Popo pull together for themselves three metal chairs. This is as far away as they can get from the eerie, glowing bug catcher electrocuting bugs, a thing worse than even the sun. Than anything.

Avery leans her broad back forward, reaching a hand out to Popo's knee, with Alma leaning in too, and Avery says, "Popo?" and it takes plain effort to say "Popo," the name is so new. "Do you want to tell me what happened?"

"I did not see anything wrong. Did you, Alma?" Popo says to Alma, who has brought over three iced teas with mint springs in frosted plastic tumblers to go with their pieces of cake.

"She was happy," Alma says.

But after thinking, she says, "She dyed her hair black, and when she got that bad flu in the winter and had to stay in bed the roots grew out, and that got her down."

"Then it started with the lateness," Popo says. "Hey, what about those kids, Avery? You better go and call them."

"What about what lateness?" Avery says.

"Well, Marian—she was always late places, ever since I knew her . . ." Alma says.

"And then it got worse," Popo says.

"How late?" Avery says.

"Well, she could be known—nobody was surprised to see her come even two hours late for bridge club," Alma says.

"What did you do?" Avery says.

"We waited for her. We would sit and talk. Some of us started coming even later, so it didn't matter much. And she was always so nice when she got there. She really was just the nicest person. Wasn't she, Popo? Nice?" Alma says.

"What did you say to her?" Avery says.

"I said nothing to her. What would we say? She was so nice," Alma says.

"Me, I would say, 'Marian, why are you late? We don't want to sit around two hours waiting for you,' " says Avery.

"We wouldn't say that, and you know you wouldn't either, Avery. You are not rude."

"Would you, Avery?" Popo says, scraping up some frosting with the side of his finger. "You probably would. She would, Alma."

"Well," Alma says, "what would that have done? What would that have gotten you? Then there would have been no bridge game at all. Our way," Alma says, collecting the plates and wandering off towards the house, "we had two hours to visit with each other and then bridge with a nice person. Your way, you just would be rocking the boat, don't you see? You get nothing."

Avery watches her, then looks down at her shoes, then at her stocking, which is bunching slightly at one ankle. She reaches

her hand down to get it to go smooth while Popo munches on
a mint leaf, taking tiny bites.

"Come on," he says. "What do you think? Let's take her
back and go on and do something ourselves, honey. I am tired
of old ladies always around."

Avery and Popo are in the borrowed car making a white
slash on black asphalt, parked as they are on the angle at the
Dairy Queen. Popo wants to see what is going on here as he
has heard they have a new machine to mix up the ice-cream
formula, and he still has vitality, he still wants to see what
everybody is doing in ice cream, even though his company has
long been sold.

The Dairy Queen is a white cinder-block building with a
little glassed-in front porch with pictures everywhere of Dairy
Queen treats in smooth shapes on top of brownies, between
cookies, with strawberries, pineapple sauce, chocolate, hot
fudge. There are chocolate-dip cones, chocolate-chocolate-dip
cones, shakes, sodas. Then also tacos, burritos, fries, burgers,
pig-in-a-blankets, chicken-in-a-basket, and more.

"Let's call those kids. We can, can't we? Just use this car
phone," he says, tapping the car phone with a thick-nailed
finger.

Avery punches out her home number with the area code and
starts talking to her oldest; his name is Benny. She says Popo
is with her, that Popo is the Indian she has always told them
existed, he is their great-grandfather, and that he wants to talk
to all the kids, so go find out who is around. Popo gets on the
phone, and when the children pick up, he goes from one to
another and says, "Do you know who I am? Have you heard
about me?"—which is how he opens each conversation—and
looking over at Avery, he says, "I do not want to scare them,

Avery, thinking they are talking to a strange old man and their mama is out of town. You know."

Avery feels heavy and slow, sitting on the side of the car where the sun shines through the windows the hardest and the air conditioning cannot make much of a difference.

Later, Popo is still going with the phone. "Now put Eurice back on, Ben," he says. "I just thought of something I want to tell her, something I forgot the first time." He leans his head back on the headrest the way Avery has her head as he waits for Ben to run and drag Eurice back to the phone.

"What kind of ice-cream bar is your favorite?" is the kind of thing Popo is saying while sitting next to Avery, speaking into the car phone and stubbing out one cigarette and right away lighting up another.

Avery's back hurts. She shifts her body around and sits hanging her arms over the steering wheel, narrowing her eyes to read the posters to herself, looking at the pictures that are everywhere on the Dairy Queen walls and windows. "What do you want?" Avery finally says.

"Hold on a minute, Anita, your mama wants to say something. What do I want?" he says to Avery.

"I mean, do you want any Dairy Queen?"

"I don't know. I will decide when I get off the phone. I want to come inside and see the whole works, how they do it, talk to them about everything."

Avery climbs out of the car and wanders around looking at the wildflowers that grow up stalky with small leaves and tiny flowers at the edge of the cinder parking lot, the cinders smelling like hot tar—at least hot-tar smell is thick in the air. If not from the cinders, it is some kind of road smell.

Inside the Dairy Queen on the little glassed-in slab of cement, she waits, slapping flies, now wanting a sweater, watching goose bumps from the freezing air conditioning pop out on her arms, in a bunched-up line with adults and kids dressed in summer shorts and T-shirts, jeans and V-necked halter tops, with almost everyone having layers cut into their hair, that is their style, and the line is so long, Avery so bored, she begins seeing artichokes, their heads looking like a field of artichokes turned upside down, some with leaves that are long and some with just baby leaves, little short spiky things thatched on their heads. She orders a marshmallow sundae and rests her elbow on the countertop to look out the window at Popo, who is still talking into the phone.

Avery, now back wandering around, back next to the Dairy Queen kitchen door, too close to the cooking vent, where there is a fly-dotted chair, a fly airport shaded by the building, a chair that is the only place she can find to go and sit and watch for some sign from Popo for her to come to him from the car.

She hears rock music from a beat box. In the kitchen, there are minimum-wage teenagers dressed in jeans and sneakers, wearing white shirts with white aprons wrapped around their waists, the straps tied in mean little nail-breaking knots. The teenagers are crisscrossing the kitchen, running into each other, pulling dripping baskets of fries out of the fat, flipping hamburgers, chopping lettuce for tacos, and Avery sits and watches them as she spoons her sundae.

One of the girls, her face and neck slick with heat, comes slipping out the door, leaning up against the wall close to Avery, her hands little fists balled in the small of her back. She has one knee bent, her foot up behind her against the cinderblock wall, her heavy hair pulled up from her face and tied with a long cotton scarf, or rag, in the way a Sandinista would wear it, behind her ears, her hair spilling over and away and off her neck. The sleeves of her shirt are rolled tight, her hipbones press out against black jeans that go down narrow to black leather clunky shoes that stream their laces. She glances at Avery and tugs the scarf from her hair to wipe it across her face the way Avery saw Popo do with the Kleenex she gave him at the funeral.

A boy, maybe nineteen years old, maybe twenty-five, comes out the kitchen door holding cold drinks and hands one to the girl. He heads over to a van parked under a tree back deep in the cinder lot, the girl following along, coltish, stumbling, kicking up cinders with her loose black shoes, and she stands, knees and elbows angled beside the boy, who puts a long arm around her neck, pulling her over toward him; he puts his cheek up against her cheek, maybe saying something, maybe kissing her neck and cheek, until the girl's body, loose as her knees, causes Avery to watch them, to simply stare. Even in their bodies there is light and bend and movement, and what roundness there is is packed over muscle and bone.

The boy and the girl get in the van and drive out of the Dairy Queen lot, passing in front of Avery, then, oddly, stopping, skidding on cinders; the backup lights light up brightly, and the van backs up. It stops in front of Avery as if they had forgotten her and were coming back to get her, Avery sitting rapt and still in the fly chair, waiting to see what will happen.

The girl jumps out, runs around the van, and stumbling and catching herself up, reaches into the kitchen door, grabbing up the beat box, what she has forgotten.

Avery sits alone looking at the tangle of living things growing up around the Dumpster, endless chain-link fence, off at the expressway, and she sees something dropped, the rag or scarf that is the girl's lying off by some weeds and crumpled papers, some smashed cups. Going over to where the scarf is lying jagged across the cinders like lightning fallen, Avery stoops to pick it up, and holding it to her face, smelling the very girl in it—it is a thick cotton—she stands off behind the Dairy Queen for a time, barely able to make out Popo, who is sitting alone in the car. The light is failing now. She drops down on the fly chair and goes to work with the scarf, wrapping it thickly around her wrist, around and around like a bracelet or a cuff, and oddly, if Popo looks up at her while he is talking, he will not know, he will not see in this light Avery smiling at him in a small way, then more broadly. She thinks, she knows, that this powwow is finally over, is a thing behind her barely to be thought about again or even remembered, and the smile is just something that bubbles up in her heart in the most natural of ways.

Just Avery, herself.

A NOTE ABOUT THE AUTHOR

Patricia Lear grew up in Memphis, Tennessee. Her home is now Kenilworth, Illinois, where she lives with her husband and their two children.

A Note on the Type

This book was set in a digitized version of Janson. The hot-metal version of Janson was a recutting made direct from type cast from matrices long thought to have been made by the Dutchman Anton Janson, who was a practicing type founder in Leipzig during the years 1668–1687. However, it has been conclusively demonstrated that these types are actually the work of Nicholas Kis (1650–1702), a Hungarian, who most probably learned his trade from the master Dutch type founder Dirk Voskens. The type is an excellent example of the influential and sturdy Dutch types that prevailed in England up to the time William Caslon (1692–1766) developed his own incomparable designs from them.

Composed by The Haddon Craftsmen,
Scranton, Pennsylvania
Printed and bound by Arcata Graphics,
Martinsburg, West Virginia
Design and computer art by Irva Mandelbaum